BODY BELOW THE BRIDGE

A murder mystery that keeps you guessing

DIANE M. DICKSON

THE BOOK FOLKS

Published by The Book Folks

London, 2024

© Diane Dickson

ISBN 978-1-80462-169-1

www.thebookfolks.com

BODY BELOW THE BRIDGE *is the seventh standalone title in the DI Jordan Carr mystery series.*

A list of characters can be found at the back of this book.

Chapter 1

The M57 isn't one of the busiest motorways in the UK. The bridge carrying Spencer's Lane over it is not impressive, compared to many other similar constructions. However, dropping from the parapet onto the carriageway in front of an articulated lorry pretty much guarantees to achieve what now lay bloodied and broken under a white police-scene tent.

By the time DI Jordan Carr joined the tailback of traffic, the delay was already approaching an hour. Drivers climbed from their stationary vehicles to peer into the distance, hoping to see the cause of the hold-up. The local radio reported the closure of the motorway with diversions from junction six.

If he'd known earlier, Jordan could have avoided the jam. Returning home after staying in Kirkby for a pre-Christmas night out, there were plenty of other routes he could have taken.

There was a meeting scheduled with his boss, DCI Josh Lewis, at Copy Lane in two hours. Jordan glanced at his watch. At this rate, there wouldn't be time to go home and change. He resisted the urge to take advantage of his position in the force for a couple of minutes longer before giving in. His own VW Golf had no police livery, so he pulled his warrant card from the glove compartment and held it open in front of the windscreen. Once on the hard shoulder, he headed towards the strobing lights and gathering of emergency vehicles.

He had assumed the hold-up was due to some sort of nasty crash, but the absence of wrecked cars and the single white plastic scene cover told a different story. A bike officer waved him to a halt.

"Oh, hello, sir. I didn't recognise you."

"No problem. What's going on?"

"It's nasty. Some poor bugger jumped from the bridge. He landed right in front of that artic. It's a mess."

"Is there anything I can do to help?" This was not a totally altruistic offer. Helping at the scene was a perfectly acceptable reason for skipping the meeting. It promised to be long and tedious, covering, as it would, finance and staffing – or rather the increasing shortages of both.

"I don't think so, sir. The medical examiner is here already, and we're trying to move things along so we can get a couple of lanes open and shift this jam." The officer waved towards the stationary vehicles.

"Is that Dr Jasper's car?" Jordan said.

"It is. Not too happy to be called this early and in this weather. It's been sleeting non-stop since he got here. Do you know him?"

"I do. I can imagine he's not in the best of moods."

"Can't be helped, can it?" The bobby raised a wry smile.

James Jasper, the medical examiner, was normally taciturn and prone to grumpiness, so the present situation would be tense at best.

Jordan could have driven away and left them to it. Later, he would wish that he had, but he was spotted by the figure ducking out from the door of the tent, already stripping off his scene suit and booties. He raised a hand as he strode across the tarmac.

"Jordan. How are you and how is that lovely wife of yours?" Jasper said.

"We're well, thank you. This is a bit of a mess, isn't it?"

"It is, but I don't know why they've sent for you. I don't think there's any mystery. Bloke dropped from the bridge. The lorry did the rest. It's so selfish. Look at the state of that poor sod." He pointed to the truck driver who was sitting in the open door of a patrol car, a silver survival blanket round his shoulders. "He'll have to carry this memory for the rest of his life now. Then there's the damage to his truck, which is going to put him off the road for a while. If you want to top yourself, do it where it won't interfere with other people."

"I was just passing and came to see if I could help at all." This was stretching the truth. Jasper wasn't easily misled and raised his eyebrows.

"Glutton for punishment, are you? Or can you just not mind your own business? Well, I don't know what you can do. We can't know what brought him to this yet, but we know how it all ended up. Anyway, I can't stand around in the rain jawing with you. I have work to do. The university is on break, and I had hoped to get away. Inevitably, one of the research students turned up with Covid, breathed all over my lot, put them on the sick, so now I've got this to deal with."

"Do you know if he's been identified?"

"Bloody hell, Carr, that's not my job. Ask the scene manager." Jasper stomped off towards his car.

Chapter 2

Jordan stood for a moment, hunched against the freezing sleet. It didn't seem that there was much he could do now. He was just getting wet and cold. He would head off, go straight to his office, and change into the suit he kept in his locker. If he got a move on, there might be time for a breakfast roll in the canteen, and he would put on the coffeemaker. He pulled out his phone to call Penny and tell his wife that he wouldn't make it home yet.

"Jordan, fancy meeting you here." Ted Bliss, the crime scene sergeant, was peering at him from deep inside the hood of a rain jacket. "They didn't drag you out as well, did they?"

"No, just chance, but this isn't your usual sort of job, is it? Are there not enough suspicious deaths in Liverpool to keep you busy?"

"Huh, I wish. It's the usual crap. Covid, winter flu, and Christmas leave. Copy Lane has been like the bloody Marie Celeste this weekend. Somebody had to handle this lot, and I used to be a traffic officer. I know they say never volunteer, but what can we do?"

"Have we got an ID?"

"Not yet. Nothing on him, no wallet or driving licence or what have you. I've got a couple of mobile officers scouting the road both ways to see if there is a car abandoned anywhere. If there's nothing, we have to assume he's from nearby."

"Could have walked, though, or hitched."

"Either of those is possible, of course, but he's not dressed for walking in this weather. Let's just hope his car is up the lane there with his wallet in it."

"Do you consider how you're dressed when you're on the way to commit suicide?" Jordan said.

"Don't ask me. I can't imagine what state you must be in to do something like that. Maybe we'll find a note and we can clear all this mess away, hand the case over to the coroner and put it behind us. I just need someone to take a proper statement from the truck driver. We also need to make sure he's got a lift home or wherever he wants to go now. There's nothing we can do for the other guy. I'd rather take care of the living."

"I'll do that, if you like."

"Are you sure? One of the bobbies can do it."

"Yes, I know, but there's a meeting back at the office about finance and staffing in…" Jordan glanced at his watch "about an hour."

"Ah. Fair enough. Be my guest then."

"Cheers, let me know if they find the victim's car. I'd like to put a name to him."

"Will do."

* * *

"How are you doing, mate?" Jordan crouched beside the open patrol car and flashed his warrant card. "It's Dave Petty, isn't it?"

The other man nodded.

"Do you want to sit inside? We can put the heater on, get you warmed up a bit."

"Thanks, but no. I want to keep an eye on my truck, and I don't very much want to sit in a cop car. No offence, but I haven't done anything wrong, and it would make me feel as if I had."

"I can understand that, but look, nothing's going to happen to your vehicle for a while, and you're certainly not going to be able to drive it away. You might as well be more comfortable. I'd like to get a statement from you and it's not very nice for either of us here. Tell you what, come on over to my car. I reckon you can see your lorry from there and it'll soon warm up with the heater on."

With a glance at the Golf, the truck driver nodded and pushed himself upright, dragging the thin silver blanket around him. He followed Jordan across the glass strewn tarmac. He was shaking with the effects of shock and Jordan wished he had a warm drink to offer him. "Do you want me to arrange for a doctor?"

"No, they already offered me that. I'm not hurt. I just can't get warm. This thing" – he rattled the blanket – "it helps, but I can't stop shivering."

"It's shock. You need a hot sweet drink and to be away from here. Do you live locally?"

"No, I've come down from Manchester. This would have been my last run before the Christmas break. It was supposed to be a quickie with a load of wood for the docks. Bloody typical. I mean, I feel sorry for the bloke but, why me?"

"Yes, it's rotten luck. How will you get home without your truck?"

"I've already rung my mate, and he's on the way. How he'll get through this lot, I don't know."

"I'll give his details to one of the bike lads and when he hits the back of the queue, they can filter him out and bring him down. You'll have to go down as far as Switch Island, but then you can turn straight round and head home. Just give me a description of his car and his registration number."

"Thanks, mate, that's decent of you."

Jordan gave the information to a traffic officer, then climbed back into his warming car.

"How are you doing?" he said.

"Better, thanks. I just want to get home."

Jordan pulled out his notebook and asked permission to record the statement on his phone. It didn't take very long. The driver had left Manchester after a good night's sleep at home. He'd had no alcohol or drugs. He'd been bowling along the relatively quiet road, looking forward to putting his truck away and having a couple of days off with the family. The crash had come out of nowhere. There had been no warning. He hadn't looked up onto the bridge. It was just an ordinary run until the windscreen shattered and there was the quick flash of colour and the knowledge that something awful had happened.

"I had hoped for a minute that it'd been kids. The little sods fling things over the rails sometimes. They don't see how lethal that can be, idiots. But it was too early, and I sort of knew what had happened even before I got out of the cab."

"Were there no other cars around at the time?"

"No, not right then. I think a couple passed just after it happened, but I don't reckon they clocked that anything had occurred. Most likely, they assumed I'd broken down.

Nobody stopped." He leaned forward and watched the activity in silence for a few moments. "Will they let me know who he was?"

"There'll be an inquest, so you will find out. Do you want to know about him?"

"I'm not sure. I suppose so. Do you know why he did it?"

"Not yet. We might well find out when we locate his car or speak to his family."

Jordan saw in the rear-view mirror the blue lights of the motorbike as it sped down the hard shoulder, followed by a dark blue Jaguar. "I reckon your mate's here now. You get off home. We'll be in touch. You'll need to sign the statement, but someone can bring it to you. If you think you need a doctor, don't hesitate. Shock can be nasty. We'll provide you with a case number for your insurance and there'll be some follow-up in the next few days, and then a date for the inquest. But try to have a good break. I know it might be difficult, but just keep in mind this wasn't your fault, Dave."

Chapter 3

By the time Dave and his mate were ready to leave, some colour had come back into the truck driver's face. He managed to smile and raise a hand in acknowledgement to Jordan as they pulled away.

Sergeant Bliss, walking across from near the scene tent, raised a plastic evidence bag in the air. "There's a white Ford Focus pulled onto the grass at the junction up there by the houses. It was unlocked, and his wallet was in the glove compartment." The driving licence, in the small plastic window, showed a picture of a white man with dark hair, and a clean-shaven jaw and just the hint of a smile. "I think we can be pretty sure this is our victim. He's pretty knocked about, but the picture on this driving licence has got to be him. Before you ask, there's just a few pounds and one bank card. No phone anywhere that we've found yet."

"Someone needs to do the knock," Jordan said, reading the address on the laminated card, and referring to the horrible job of notifying next of kin.

"I'll arrange that," Bliss said. "Unless you fancy the job. It's on your way back to Copy Lane."

"I can't say I fancy it, but I can take it on. Will you arrange for a liaison officer to attend?"

"I will. I owe you, Jordan. It's rotten, but it'll be the quickest way. Apart from that, you can reassure the family that we're looking after him. Not much to do in that line, but if you've been here, it'll be more convincing."

There was nothing more to keep him, and the weather was worsening. Wind whipped icy sleet into their faces and there was no sign of a let-up. Jordan was glad of an excuse to leave.

The car was overly warm and muggy. Jordan threw his waterproof jacket onto the back seat, turned the heater off, and pulled into the nearside lane. A vehicle transporter passed on the other side of the motorway, heading to the accident site. Soon, the road would be cleared, all evidence of the terrible death of Stanley Lipscowe would be removed. No doubt some drivers would speculate. If they read the *Echo* later, or listened to Radio Merseyside, they would tell their friends, "I was there. Held us up for ages."

* * *

The house was a semi. The walls were pebble-dashed and the front garden was paved with flagstones. It was no different from dozens of others in the area. Some had extensions on the side, some had dormer windows, but they were all basically the same ex-council properties. They were built in the sixties for workers in the short-lived economic boom.

Jordan parked illegally with two wheels on the kerb. He didn't think anyone would take issue with it this early, the roads were still almost deserted. Schools had already finished for the holidays and the foul weather was keeping everyone indoors.

He pressed the small, illuminated bell push twice. There was no answer. There was no car parked in the front area. He wondered if Stanley lived alone. That would be a minor complication because they needed to find a next of kin. He rapped with his knuckles on the shiny black paint. Still no response. He bent to peer through the letter box flap. "Hello, anybody in?" he shouted.

"Hey, what are you doing?" He twisted round, but there was no one behind him.

"Up here."

A woman's face poked out from an upstairs window in the house next door. She had on what appeared to be a plastic shower cap and, as she spoke, she dragged the collar of a thick dressing gown closer to her neck.

"Stan's not in, his car's gone, and Tracy won't be up yet."

Jordan held up his warrant card. "DI Jordan Carr. Is Tracy Mr Lipscowe's partner?"

"Aye, his wife. But like I say, she won't be up. She doesn't get up till her carer comes. Probably be another hour at least. Though you never can tell these days. They're so run off their feet, you just don't know when they'll make it. Sometimes not at all."

"What happens then?"

"There's that key box thingy screwed on the wall. I go in of a morning when I can and make her a cuppa and a bit of toast. Sometimes we have a jangle if I've got time. Not today, though. I'm off down the shops to finish my shopping for Crimbo. I was just going in the shower." This reminded her about her headwear, which she dragged off. She ran fingers through her blond, curly hair. "What's to do, anyway? Why are the police coming round?"

"I'm afraid there's been an incident and I need to speak to her. Do you think you could help? Could you come down and let me in?"

"Oh, soddin' hell. Yes, I suppose so. Just hang on there a bit. I'll need to put me clothes on. Bloody great this is, and me meeting our Jackie in an hour."

The woman brought with her a piece of notepaper with the code number scribbled on it. She tapped at the keypad, lifted the black plastic cover, and removed the key. "Tracy, it's me, Flo. I've let meself in. Are you decent, love? There's a copper here wants a word." As she yelled out, she crossed the square hallway and placed a foot on the bottom stair. "Alright if I come up? Hello, Tracy." There was no reply, and Flo glanced back at Jordan. "Best if you stay here, lad. She might be still asleep. She takes pills that knock her out. I wouldn't want her to be embarrassed."

Jordan nodded, closed the door, and stood with his back against the wall.

The thick carpet cushioned Flo's footsteps as she climbed to the upper floor. At the top, a stairlift was folded back against the wall.

He heard her tap on the bedroom door and call out, "Cooee. I'm coming in, love. It's just me." There was the click of a latch and the soft creak of floorboards overhead. To give Flo her due, the neighbour didn't scream out. She didn't panic or fuss. She simply appeared on the landing, leaned a little so that she could look Jordan in the eye, and said, "You'd better come up, lad. I don't reckon you'll be talking to Tracy today."

Chapter 4

Florence McGrady brought a couple of mugs of tea and a box holding mince pies from her home. Jordan had made some phone calls to start the ball rolling. Now, while they waited in the hallway, the neighbour provided refreshments. She had rejected Jordan's suggestion that she wait in her own place. "It's not right leaving Tracy on her own. I know you'd be here, but you're nothing to her. She was my mate, poor love. I'll stay till you tell me I have to go away."

Eating mince pies and drinking coffee in the hallway with a dead body just yards away upstairs felt surreal. But Flo had been helpful, and to refuse seemed churlish. The sugar and carbs helped clear Jordan's mild hangover, and the drink was counteracting the chill as his damp clothes began to dry.

Upstairs, Tracy Lipscowe lay in disarray. The thick quilt in its pink flowered cover had slid to the floor and the white sheet underneath was crumpled and twisted. Jordan had left Florence on the landing while he went as far as the bed to check for signs of life. There were none. He surveyed the space. Side tables flanked a double bed in the centre of the room. One of them held medications and a box of tissues. On the other was a small tablet computer and some spectacles. A pair of soft trousers and a thick jumper were thrown across the back of a chair. There was a small trolley holding bottles and jars. A row of built-in wardrobes covered one wall. There was no sign that a man shared the room. He glanced into the bathroom, which had grab handles fitted, and a walk-in shower with a plastic chair inside. A small room at the back, overlooking the garden, was where Stanley had slept. Jeans and a hoody were in a heap on the floor. Men's trainers were pushed into a corner. The headboard was dark wood and the bed linen was plain white. The dresser top was bare and everywhere was tidy.

Downstairs, Jordan glanced into the living room and kitchen. There was no clutter. A couple of interior doors had been removed, presumably to allow ease of movement for the walking frame which stood in the corner of the dining room. The only thing that could be described as clutter was a small artificial Christmas tree beside the fireplace. There were a few wrapped gifts underneath and trimmings, some of which looked old and often used; family memories in glass and glitter.

"Had you known her very long?" Jordan asked as they crossed the landing. He wanted to take Florence's mind from the scene.

"Oh aye, ever since we moved in over twenty years ago. We were all a lot younger and a lot thinner then." Flo tried to laugh away the tears that had gathered in her eyes, but they overflowed. Jordan turned away to give her privacy for a couple of seconds. "She was fit then, of course. That was before the MS cursed her. She used to look after my Jackie sometimes. Never had no kids of her own. I don't think she wanted any, truth be told. She worked on a babywear stall in St John's Market. Loved it, she did, but she didn't want the bother of kids. It's gone now, the stall. That place is not a patch on what it was. Stan worked in the printers. He earned good money. He took redundancy and now works part-time so he can be with Trace. They were always off on foreign holidays and what have you, so you can't blame her for wanting it to just be the two of them. Poor Stan. Will you be the one that has to tell him? Oh, you never said what the incident was. I hope it's nothing serious. He's going to have enough to cope with now, poor bugger."

"You wouldn't know when she last saw the doctor, would you?"

"Yes. She went to the hospital about a year ago, and she saw Doctor Khan in September. She was overdue to see him again, but with Christmas and the waiting lists, she couldn't get an appointment. I always go with her, and we go for a coffee or maybe a drink afterwards. It made her feel normal, ordinary. You have to understand. She didn't sit and mope. Yes, sometimes she got fed up, don't we all? But she lived life. She went out and had a laugh and just coped really well. We were due to go in the new year. Does it matter?"

"It could do. If she hasn't seen the doctor for a while and they didn't expect this to happen. It makes a difference to the way we handle things."

"Oh. The last time they said she was doing okay. To carry on with the pills and whatnot. Mind you, their idea of doing okay isn't mine, but I suppose that doesn't matter now. Poor Trace, I'm really going to miss her being here."

"How long had she been ill?"

"It was slow at first, so I don't know exactly, but for about two years she's had to use the frame and the wheelchair. Stan takes her out, pushes her around, but she can do it herself. She was going to get herself an electric one next year. Said I'd have to run to keep up with her then. Maybe her going now is a blessing. He's still quite young, isn't he? Perhaps he'll be able to still have some life, you know, after he gets over it."

Jordan couldn't let her continue without saying something. "I'm sorry, Flo. Stan died this morning."

"Aw, God no. That's terrible. Did he have a heart attack? I know he had pills for his blood pressure."

"I'm not able to tell you much just now. Sorry."

She paused for a few minutes, digesting the information. "I suppose, in a way, we could see it as the best thing. You know, Tracy never knowing. But he was still so young." Now, quite suddenly, the news was too much, and Flo began to sob.

Jordan's instinct was to wrap his arms around her, but he held back, as he knew he must, muttering comforting noises and feeling useless.

Now they stood waiting in the quiet hallway and ate celebration pastries, and tried to think of things to say.

It was a relief when the medical examiner's car and the coroner's van arrived.

Chapter 5

Dr Jasper stomped into the hallway, where Jordan waited. "This is beyond a joke. My wife has already gone to the cottage in Wales. Her car's loaded up with food and even a bloody wreath for the door. She will not be happy if I don't join her in time to trim the tree. Bloody hell, Jordan, are you wasting my time? A sick woman dying. Surely it doesn't need all this. It'd better not be a lot of fuss about nothing. Couldn't it wait?"

Jordan apologised, though why he should do wasn't clear. But there was no harm in smoothing the waters. He gave Dr Jasper a quick rundown of the situation but steered clear of voicing all his ideas. The medical examiner would make up his own mind without hearing what a policeman thought.

With a humph, the medic thumped up the stairs, his scene suit rustling as he left.

Jordan was itching to get back to the station. In his gut, he knew there was something off here. He must wait, though, until Jasper came back. Just in case he'd misjudged the situation.

Jasper was quieter when he rejoined Jordan by the door. "You saw the petechia?"

The way to handle Jasper was to give him due deference. Jordan told him he thought he had detected the tiny burst blood vessels around Tracy's eyes but hadn't been sure. Jasper nodded and sighed. "I suppose you want the examination unreasonably quickly?"

"Did they tell you she was the wife of the motorway victim?"

"Ah, no. That would make you think maybe a murder-suicide, I expect?"

Jordan shrugged. It had been his first thought and made a sort of tragic sense. But that would be jumping to the easiest conclusion. "I'll get a scene manager and the SOCO team down here and we'll get things started," he said. "I wonder if Ted Bliss is still stuck on the M57."

"No idea, and that's not my problem, is it? I'll get back to my place and make a start on the husband. That'll clear the decks, so I'll be ready for this lady. Jordan…" Jasper waited to be sure he had Jordan's full attention. "Don't bring me any more. Mrs Jasper is not to be trifled with at this time of the year." With that, he pulled off his scene suit, stuffed it into a plastic bag with the booties and mask and without a further word stormed to his car and slammed the door.

Jordan called Stella May at Copy Lane and filled her in on the details. He asked her to let DC John Grice know and prepare things, but he added the rider that he hoped it would be over quickly and that it wouldn't interfere with anyone's plans for the next weekend.

Back in the incident room, everyone was of the same opinion as the medical examiner. John said that he wasn't cancelling his leave because, surely, this was going to be straightforward and cleared up in a day or two. Just dotting 'i's and crossing 't's. Sad but simple.

Stella had the record books ready and handed them out. "Waste of paper," John said.

Jordan poured a mug of coffee and walked to the front of the room. "I know this appears to be simple. I know we all want that to be the case because of the timing, but I have a couple of reservations. So, let's just hold off making any assumptions until we have reports from the morgue and the SOCO team."

"But, boss," John said, sounding a little desperate, "we're not going to have any DNA or toxicology results until after Christmas."

"There'll still be things we can do in the meantime. We all know that the first days are the most important and that doesn't change just because of a national holiday."

"I've booked to go away, boss. I'm taking Millie."

It was the first time John had referred to his relationship with a colleague from the technical lab. The inevitable cat calls and gestures greeted the comment.

John snorted and glared at the room in general.

"Sorry, John," Jordan said, "but she knows the score, doesn't she? She's part of the force."

"That's not the point, boss."

There was no benefit in entering a discussion about it. John hadn't been a detective for very long. He still hadn't quite learned that booking trips and planning events didn't guarantee that they would happen.

Chapter 6

The conference table in DCI Josh Lewis's office held platters of snacks. There were bottles and glasses on a cabinet against the wall. A tiny Christmas tree with flashing lights was on top of his filing cabinet and the secretary, Karen, was setting out two coffee pots. She smiled and raised her eyebrows as she passed Jordan in the doorway.

"Try to make it quick, Jordan. I've got visitors in a quarter of an hour. The leader of the council, people from

Rotary and the Chamber of Commerce. Networking. It's boring but has to be done. I was going to ask you to join us, but now there's this."

It was unlikely that he had been an intended guest at the gathering. Jordan suspected the two deaths had been a relief to Lewis, who now had a good excuse to leave him off the guest list.

"Sorry, sir. Can't be helped, can it?"

"I've seen your report. Looks cut and dried. The husband killed his wife in what he thought was an act of kindness and then threw himself in front of a truck. Terrible, terrible. But shouldn't take too long to clear up."

Everyone had already reached the same conclusion, and it would be easy to agree and simply go through the motions. Jordan had questions, though. There were things that didn't sit right with him.

"I'll keep you informed, sir."

"Bear in mind the time of the year, we don't want to pay overtime if we can avoid it. Everything is going to take longer than normal at the labs and whatnot."

"Yes, I realise that. I'll keep it in mind."

Jordan left the chief inspector's office irritated by the constant reference to cost. It was understandable given the pressure the force was under, but there was also the Christmas hysteria, which wasn't. If you celebrated what he had always thought was supposed to be the true meaning of the whole religious thing, it was one day, maybe two. But nowadays, the world ground to a halt for a week or more and everyone accepted it. No, they expected it. But Tracy and Stanley Lipscowe were just as dead as they would have been in February or the middle of June. It was going to be an uphill struggle, but this case had to be given the same attention as any other.

When he arrived in the incident room, there was a sudden pause in the conversation. They were moaning among themselves, weren't they? He tapped on his desk to attract the team's attention.

"Okay, listen. I know we could say this is the worst time for a murder, but truly, there's never a good time. This is not the first Christmas act of violence. We all know that. We have a week before the holiday, and we could be lucky and wind this up rapidly. But there'll be no shortcuts, no sloppy detective work. Not in my team. I understand that you're all anxious about plans, but let's just concentrate on the job in hand and hope for the best." He didn't wait for any response. "Stella, can I have a word?"

Jordan left the room and walked along the corridor to the small office with his name on the door. The window had a view of the car park, and the chair had a dodgy castor. He perched on the corner of the desk.

When Detective Sergeant Stella May joined him, she showed no sign of being anxious or put out and he wondered what her plans were for the festive season.

He told her what he had noticed in the house belonging to the Lipscowes and why it was bothering him. She thought for a while and then nodded. She got it and he felt some of the tension leave his shoulders.

"They'll be fine, boss," she said. "You know that, don't you? Once we get into it, they'll settle. I think everyone was getting into a party mood and this has been a bit of a downer but, yes, they'll be fine. Mind you, we won't have Kath Webster. She's got an appointment for her knee operation. She goes in on Tuesday."

"We'll miss her. How long will she be on sick for?"

"About six weeks, if all goes well."

"Hopefully, we'll sort this long before then."

"Well, the sooner we get started, the better the chances. What's the first move?"

The neighbour had told Jordan that as far as she knew, the only living relative was an aunt who lived in Wales and she would need to be told as a matter of urgency. Stella had set up the room and had the computer generate an operational name. They would both go to the post-mortem exam later in the afternoon. DC John Grice was tasked with contacting the hospital and speaking to the dead woman's GP for as many details as they were willing to share. Data protection no longer applied, but medical people were notoriously unwilling to talk about their patients.

Jordan called Penny. She would know quickly that their Christmas plans were under threat, but she'd cope. She always did.

Chapter 7

Dr Jasper was already clattering about in the examination room when Stella and Jordan arrived at the Liverpool City Mortuary. The university was already closed for the holidays, and the campus buildings were quiet. The mortuary assistant grinned at them as they left the changing room. "He's in a foul mood. Best if you say as little as possible." The twinkle in the woman's eyes made it plain that she was used to working with Jasper and his temper hadn't fazed her at all. "On the upside, he hasn't thrown anything, but he's doing a lot of muttering under his breath. Go on in. I'll be in shortly. He's finished the exam on the poor bloke from the motorway and now he's onto your lady."

Jasper glanced up as they took their places against the wall. "Oh, made it, did you? I was about to start, couldn't wait any longer. I'm off to Wales tonight no matter what, and I intend to arrive before my wife and her sister get into the brandy."

Jordan apologised and hated that he felt the need, but the medical examiner had the same effect on just about everyone. "Your technician said you'd done with Stanley Lipscowe."

"Yes, that's why I'm later than planned with this lady. We need to talk afterwards. But let's just get on with this and stop blathering."

It was never pleasant to stand by and watch as the body of a human was sliced and dissected, the internal organs weighed, and samples taken for testing. Jordan and Stella had both been through the ordeal before. They had experienced the whine of the saw, the smells, and the sounds. The only thing to do was to tune out the horror and concentrate on the commentary. Of course, it would all be in reports but hearing Jasper's descriptions and thoughts at times, such as this, with the victim laid before them on the table, they both found that it concentrated the mind in a way that reading cold facts could not.

There was nothing all that unforeseen. He confirmed there were fibres in the nose and mouth and he expected to find them in the lungs when they were dissected. He suggested they would more than likely match those taken from the covers of the pillow found beside the bed. It had been a foregone conclusion really and saddeningly unsurprising. Tracy had been suffocated. They'd taken samples for toxicology testing, but Jasper was of the opinion that she was sedated before she was killed. "There is residue of pills in her stomach. We need to know when she normally took them and that will give us an idea of the time of death."

Jordan frowned as he made a note to speak to Flo and see if she knew Tracy's routine so intimately.

Jasper invited them into his office. As they left the technician replacing Tracy's organs and stitching up the Y incision, Jordan took Stella aside. "Did anyone interview the carer?"

Stella shook her head. "Not as far as I know. I'll have to review the reports, but I'm not sure she even turned up. Mind you, if she saw all the palaver at the house, it wouldn't be surprising that she swerved it. The evening visit would have been cancelled when the care company was told she was dead, I expect. I'll check it all. Oh, by the way, it's Operation Song Thrush. A bit poetic for a murder, but that's what was generated by the computer."

"Okay, noted. We need to get on with interviewing the carer as soon as. Can you do it and ask about the medication routine as well as all the usual? How she was, how the hubby was, and whatnot. Do it tonight if possible. I know it's getting late. By telephone will suffice, with follow-up in person whenever. Do you reckon Jasper'll pop into the aunty's on his way to the holiday cottage? She lives in Wales."

Stella gave a laugh and shook her head. "Possibly not. The local police are dealing with it. They are going to bring her through if necessary to do the formal ID. We should have some information by now. If not, we'll default to the neighbour."

Stella mentally re-arranged her plans for the evening. Her mum wouldn't be happy hearing she wasn't going round to help her with decorating the house and the tree. She was already in her black book for refusing the Boxing Day lunch invite. More than anything, what she needed was time to herself. Just a day without the forced jollity of Christmas with her brother and his partner, their little boy and whichever aunties and uncles turned up. Since the lottery win, relatives that had only been names as she'd been growing up had started to attend every gathering. People she only saw at weddings and funerals were now regular guests at her mum's new house. They used to drink cheap Australian white wine and party kegs of beer. Now they'd all developed a taste for champagne and designer brews. It wasn't that she minded, and she was strong when they approached her for loans and help with wacky ideas but, despite every effort, the win had changed things. Her job was the constant in her life, and she clung to it like a lifeline even when, as now, it was going to be tedious and more than likely upsetting.

She didn't even know what company provided the care, and the afternoon was almost over. Trying to speak to people at the council was a challenge and it being so late in the day compounded the problem. It was all going to be complicated by timing. More than anything, she wanted a long soak in the bath and a glass of wine. It wasn't happening for a while yet, though.

James Jasper surprised them by pulling from his cupboard a bottle of sherry and three glasses. "Don't think this is going to be a habit, but it's Christmas time after all, and I'm about to spoil your evening." He poured three generous measures and settled himself behind his desk.

He dismissed the examination they had just witnessed with a wave of his hand and promised that the report would be with them as soon as possible. "You missed the important part," he said as he raised his eyebrows.

Jordan didn't ask. He judged it best to give Jasper the floor. The doctor was obviously relishing his moment as he sipped at the glass of pale cream. "Your man from the M57," he said, "he had some surprises for us. It really was most interesting. It's probably going to complicate this case somewhat. I'm sorry, but the facts are the facts."

He didn't look sorry. He just looked faintly smug.

Chapter 8

Jordan called DCI Lewis as they left the centre of the city and caught him on his way home. The chief inspector sighed expansively. Jordan imagined him screwing up his eyes the way he did when something irritated him. He had no choice but to agree the investigation had taken on a different slant and a quick wind-up was now less likely.

Back at Copy Lane, the room was busy. The civilian staff had found a couple of desks one of the other teams nicked at some point and brought them back. Technicians had finished connecting computers and phones. Jordan messaged John Grice and made it plain that he expected everyone to stay if they could, as there had been important developments. It was past end of shift when Jordan and Stella arrived. No one had gone home.

There was one obviously empty chair but a brown leather handbag showed that Violet Purcell had turned up along with the other regulars. With only five years until retirement, Violet was happy she'd only ever reached the rank of detective constable. She maintained that she didn't want the responsibilities of rank but simply to do the job. Her family of three girls and four grandchildren were more important than professional advancement. Reliable, dogged and determined, her type was the backbone of the force and Jordan valued her. She had nipped out and bought some boxes of mince pies and a stollen. It wasn't a festive atmosphere exactly, and the general mood was more focused.

First, Jordan related the facts regarding Tracy. Her picture was already on the whiteboard. Stella made notes underneath and told them that copies of the report would be on their computers as soon as it was available.

Jordan moved to stand next to the image of Stanley Lipscowe. "I will send this report around when I have it. But the gist of it is that Stanley had extensive damage consistent with his violent death. Nothing surprising there. However, Dr Jasper also found old wounds, which he believes are pre-mortem. Bruising, a couple of wounds on his face and head. Most significantly, there were ligature marks on his wrists."

Stella was multitasking. She was attempting to trace the carer and speaking to the vehicle section to ensure someone had collected Stanley Lipscowe's car. She let the car pound know they would need to have it forensically examined. It could be a bit late now that they would have loaded it onto a transporter and driven it to the yard, but they had to go through the motions.

Jordan took Violet Purcell with him to speak to Flo.

She sat beside him in the car, quietly reading the preliminary report from the mortuary on her tablet.

Flo invited them into a house that was obviously ready for Christmas. The tree was artificial but looked expensive. There were piles of presents underneath, holly tucked behind the frames of the mirrors and pictures on the walls. She glanced around as they walked into the living room. "It seems wrong. I trimmed up Saturday and then all this happened. I almost took it down, but I changed my mind. The family's coming round and it's not their fault, is it?"

"There's no reason for you to spoil your Christmas," Vi said. "I'm sure Tracy wouldn't want that."

"No, perhaps not. I don't know what to do with them." She pointed to a little pile of parcels pulled aside. "I'd got them for Tracy and Stan. We always give each other a bit of something. Just something cheap. I bought her a scarf and some gloves. She felt the cold sitting in the wheelchair. I bought Stan a woolly hat. It's a bit daft, with a duck on it."

"Perhaps you could just give them to a homeless person. If you don't want to let any of your own relatives have them," Vi said.

"That's a boss idea. Tell you what. Why don't I give them to you? You must come into contact with rough sleepers."

"I don't much personally, but I can pass them on to the people that do."

Flo's eyes filled with tears as she handed over the packages. "Poor Trace, she didn't get a very good deal, all told, did she?" She blew her nose and visibly pulled herself together. "Anyway, what's to do now?"

Jordan asked her about the neighbours' routine, whether she was aware of when Tracy took her medication, details that could seem insignificant until they were viewed with other information. He asked if she had seen Stanley in the last few days.

"No, I hadn't seen him for a bit. He was out early, and I've got my part-time job at the nursery. I pop in to see Trace regular or give her a ring or whatever, but sometimes I didn't see Stan for a couple of weeks at a time. In the winter, I mean. In the summer, we'd natter in the garden or on the path. Didn't see him today, nor yesterday. It's a busy time of the year; last time I saw Tracy was Friday."

She hadn't seen the carer. "They used to be more regular, at one time. You knew when they'd come and who it would be. Now, though, with bloody Brexit and then the pandemic, they are really short-staffed. Same as us at the nursery. You never know who it's going to be or if they're going to turn up at all. It drove Tracy mad. She was always talking about stopping the council ones and paying for private. I don't think she could afford it, though." She paused for a moment and closed her eyes. "I never gave it much thought when we found her like that. Went clean out of my head. She either never came or she came and went away when she saw the police cars. I don't want to speak out of turn and I'm not racist, I'm truly not, but…"

They waited and eventually Flo voiced the opinion that most of the care workers were foreign, and she had wondered if they were all legal. She couldn't explain her reasoning and Jordan decided it was more to do with the media and urban myth than fact. It was obvious, though, that she wasn't going to be of much more help.

"Is there anyone else Stan might have talked to or seen recently? Does he have friends he meets up with?" Jordan asked.

"Not really. He didn't have a lot of time for that sort of thing, with Tracy needing him. There's just the bloke he works with, I suppose. It's a little print shop over in Walton."

"Do you know the name or anything?" Vi asked.

"Yes, hang on. They did invites for my sister's fortieth anniversary. I've got the bill here somewhere."

Vi checked the internet on her tablet once they were back in the car. Better Print was closed until the next morning. "Find out where the owner lives. I want to speak to him tonight if we can," Jordan said.

It turned out that Musa Rahanov lived above his shop. "Is that name Russian?" Jordan asked.

"Sounds like it. Let me have a look here." Vi clicked and scrolled on the tablet. "Ah, not Russia, Eastern Europe and Central Asia it looks like."

"Okay, let's assume he speaks English. He's running a business, after all. I don't want interpreters if we can help it."

Walton Vale, the stretch of the A59 between Orrell Park and the Black Bull pub, is a busy two-lane road lined on either side with shops, some of which have flats above them. Everything is there: restaurants, supermarkets, bars, boutiques, nail bars, and tattoo parlours. A whole gamut of small businesses. The printers had a shop front with a flat above. The accommodation was accessed via a side street and back entrance, which was narrow and unlit. Light leaked from the windows of the residential spaces above. They counted down the entrances to find the likely place in the terrace. It was all in darkness. They hammered on the door. Vi phoned the number on the letterhead Flo had given them. There was no sound of a phone ringing inside the flat. An answering machine told them to leave a message.

It had been a long, hard day, and it felt like they had achieved all that they could. Jordan rang the station and told the team they might as well go home and regroup early the next morning. He scheduled an update meeting at half past seven. Leaving Vi next to her Vauxhall in the car park, he turned straight round and set off home. He had missed the chance to give Harry his bath and bedtime story. He was hungry, jaded and badly in need of a whisky.

Chapter 9

A good night's sleep was all that Jordan needed. He was up at six and took Penny a cup of coffee while she was still in bed reading to Harry. He brought her up to date as much as he could. "I don't know what the impact will be on the Christmas plans. We'll be lucky if we're clear before next weekend. I still think you should carry on. Go on down to London on Friday and I'll join you when I can. It will devastate Nana Gloria if she doesn't have Harry to spoil."

"This is a bit of a bugger," Penny said.

"Yes, I know, and we'd cleared a lot of the ongoing stuff, or at least had it under control for the duration," Jordan said.

"It can't be helped, and we're better off than that poor couple. Fingers crossed anyway. Will you come even if it's only for the day?"

"If I can, of course. Even if it's late Christmas Eve."

* * *

Everyone was in the incident room except Kath Webster. It was obvious she wouldn't be heavily involved. They didn't blame her for having a couple more hours' sleep; most of them were envious.

The local force in Wales had contacted Tracy's aunty. She was driving through from Colwyn Bay to meet Stella at the mortuary.

"I had a quick word on the phone. I don't think she's too cut up. She's planning on going shopping after. She said they weren't close. I think that's weird, though," said Stella.

The council had eventually been persuaded to disclose the name of the company assigned the contract for the care of Tracy Lipscowe. "I'm speaking to them this morning. I'll go over there to Litherland and then head straight into town," she said.

John had spoken to the medics, and they confirmed what they already knew and nothing more. As far as they could discover, there had been no significant changes to the norm.

Vi and Jordan left for the print shop and the rest of the team settled down to a morning of watching CCTV. It wasn't exciting, but at least they were dry and warm. They needed to trace the route Stanley Lipscowe had taken to the motorway. As it was early in the morning with no school runs, it could be relatively easy assuming he had left his own home in Aintree. If not, then the whole thing would be more difficult. They would need to work backwards.

Jordan wasn't going to micromanage it. He knew the team was capable and familiar with the job. He asked John to make sure that when Kath arrived, she was put onto it. "She's brilliant with that stuff," he said.

When they got to Walton Vale, Jordan parked in the side street, and they walked back to the printers. The lights inside were on, but there was no sign of any staff. The door was locked. Jordan turned away and glanced up and down the street. "We could go round to the back. It's still a bit early. If we question him in his home, though, he'll be fussing about opening up. Let's nip across the road, grab a coffee in that place over there, and watch until nine. If he's not open by then, we'll go to the flat. Come on, I'll treat you to a Danish pastry."

They had barely settled at the little table in the window when a figure appeared behind the counter in the shop opposite. "Shall we take this with us?" Vi asked.

"No, he's not going anywhere. Even if he does, we've got a bead on him. Let's give him time to get organised. If he's relaxed, we'll get more out of him. He's our best bet for finding out how Stanley was in the last couple of weeks. He could be important. Go on, eat your bun."

Chapter 10

The small bell fastened at the top of the door jangled as Vi pushed it open. Musa Rahanov glanced up from the letter he was reading and lifted his chin, peering down his nose at the warrant card Jordan had in his hand.

"Police, in my shop. I've done nothing."

"Mr Rahanov? That is you, isn't it?" Jordan said.

"Why are you asking something you already know? You are the police. You know who I am."

This was not getting off to the relaxed and friendly start Jordan had been hoping for. He persevered. "We won't keep you long, I hope. We have a couple of questions about a man who works here. Stanley Lipscowe."

"I don't know if he works here."

Puzzled, Jordan wasn't sure how to respond. "Just to be clear, can you confirm you are Musa Rahanov, owner of this business?"

The other man took a huge white handkerchief from his pocket to wipe at his jowls and bristly chin. "It's my business, yes. I have paid my taxes. I have all my papers."

"Believe me, Mr Rahanov, we're not bringing any trouble," Vi said.

He frowned at her as if he had just noticed she was there.

"You cannot bring trouble. I have done nothing wrong."

This was getting very sticky and confusing. Jordan went for the bare facts to call a halt to the back and forth. "Mr Lipscowe is dead."

There was a silence for several moments. Rahanov's gaze flicked between Jordan and Vi.

The shopkeeper shook his head and used the handkerchief to blow his nose noisily and dab at his eyes. He told them that, now, he felt guilty. When Lipscowe had failed to turn up for work at what was one of the busiest times of the year, he had been angry assuming his employee had waited to receive his Christmas bonus and left without notice.

"When was the last time Stanley was at work?"

"Not for Thursday and Friday last week. At first, I thought his wife was ill. She had something that made her ill. I was surprised. Until then, he'd never let me down."

"How long had he worked for you?" Jordan asked.

"More than one year. Just one year in November."

"Did you notice anything odd about his behaviour recently?"

"Yes, he did not come to work."

Jordan took a breath. "Okay. But before then, was he nervous, sad, different? Did he seem worried?"

Musa pulled his thick lips downward and shook his big head slowly. "He was the same. Sometimes he worried about his wife, sometimes he was angry with her."

"Do you know why he was angry with his wife?" Vi said.

"He said she would not tell him when she was sick, when she had pain and he was…" He paused for a moment, screwing up his eyes and frowning. "I don't know the word – not angry violent but angry sad. Maybe love angry."

"Frustrated?" Jordan said.

"Yes, yes. That word. He said he was frustrated. He wanted to care for her, and she was stubborn. My wife is stubborn, I know this word. Women are stubborn."

"Did you think they were happy together? Despite Mrs Lipscowe being ill, did they seem happy?"

Musa shrugged his shoulders. "How can I know? Stanley works for me. He tells me his wife is ill and sometimes he is frustrated." He nodded as he remembered the word. "Happy. Who can tell?"

They hadn't got very far, except they knew that something had kept Stanley away from work. Tracy hadn't mentioned it to her friend. Did she not know? The car had been missing from the drive. Tracy hadn't seen Stanley. They had more information, but it hadn't told them much of value.

They drove back to Copy Lane in silence. When they walked into the incident room, it was to find a group gathered around Kath and the woman herself in floods of tears.

Chapter 11

Stella glanced across the room, grimaced. Jordan jerked his head towards the corridor. *Meet me outside.*

"What's happened?" he asked.

"The poor thing, she's in bits," said Stella. "They cancelled her operation."

"Cancelled? But she can hardly walk some days."

"Yeah, I probably should have said postponed, but the reality is they can't tell her when it'll be rescheduled. With Christmas and the waiting lists, and shortage of staff and all of that, they've just said they'll be in touch to give her a date later. She's shattered, Jordan."

"Do you think she should go home?"

"I asked her, and she said she nearly didn't come in. The letter was waiting for her last night at home. All she's done since is see-saw between rage and despair. At least here she's got company."

"I'll have a word when things in there calm down a bit," Jordan said.

"There's nothing we can do but be supportive and keep her busy, I suppose. Talking of that, I can give you an update if you have time now."

"Yep. We didn't get all that far at the printers; I'll fill you in on that. But first, what have you got for me?"

"I spoke to the care company. It was confusing, but I think maybe it's a move forward. It raises some questions, at least. The woman told me they hadn't sent a carer to the Lipscowes' address for at least a month," Stella said.

"Flo didn't give me that impression. She definitely said there were carers."

"Apparently, the couple had cancelled the contract with them. The reason they gave was they weren't happy with the service. They reported them to the council for lateness and staff not turning up, and not having enough time to do all they needed to. A whole litany of niggles. They refused to pay the last bill, and the council is investigating. The manager of the care company was really upset. She understands the problem, and it's just getting worse and worse. The people that work for her are burned out, despairing and frustrated because they know they aren't doing a good job. It's a nightmare, apparently."

"So, what were the Lipscowes doing?"

"Don't know, but didn't Flo say that Tracy had wanted to use a private company, independent of the council?"

"Yes, but they couldn't afford it. Ha, this opens up another set of questions. I'm sure you've thought of most things already."

"It's a puzzle, and there's got to be an explanation. I expect we need to go back to have a word with Flo McGrady in the house next door."

"Yes. Also, we need a look at the bank accounts. Both Tracy's and Stanley's. If they were paying for care, it will show up somewhere. It's not cheap."

Stella went back to update the board and get ready for a trip to Aintree.

Jordan peered into the room. "I'll just go and…" He waved towards the corner where Kath had her desk.

He pulled a chair to where Kath was viewing CCTV footage and making notes. "Good to see you on that. You're the best here at spotting stuff. And before you say anything, that's not me just being nice. I heard about what happened, but I need you right now so, though I am really annoyed and sorry, I can see the upside. The Lipscowes had a security camera. I don't know how good it was or even if it was working. Sergeant Flowers is on the case. It'll be going to the digital forensic department, but if they find any footage on his computer, they are going to make sure you have a copy as soon as. You've come up trumps with this stuff before."

"Thanks for that, boss. I appreciate it. I wasn't going to come in, but this job is important to me. That's why I'm so pissed off. I need to be fit to work at full pelt. I used to keep up. It's horrible to see people going out and I have to stay here because I'm just not fit enough. I've been on light duties for ages, and I feel useless sometimes."

"You're certainly not that. Did they give you no clue how long you have to wait?"

"No. The thing is, we were really chuffed with it coming up now. My daughter added her annual holiday to her Christmas break. I was going there for the first couple of weeks when they discharged me. She was all geared up to look after me. She even had grab handles fitted in the bathroom. Now she's got holiday she can't cancel, it's all wasted. She can't go away or anything at this time of the year, so she'll just be sitting at home. I don't know how I'll manage if I come out of hospital, on my own. She'll have to be at work. It's just a mess and there's nothing I can do about it." The outpouring was too much. Tears ran down Kath's face, to be wiped away with a scrappy piece of tissue.

"Oh, bloody hell. I'm sorry, boss." With that, she pushed up from the chair and limped off towards the ladies.

Jordan looked around the room. He caught Vi's eye. He waved to her and pointed to the corridor.

"That went well, not," Jordan said to Stella, as Vi led Kath to the corner by the coffeemaker and started putting together drinks for them both.

"Don't worry, boss. It wasn't you that upset her. It was the system and all the other crap that's going on. She'll be okay. She's tough," Stella said.

"Yes, I know, but she shouldn't need to be. You can feel the atmosphere in the room. Everybody feels sorry and awkward."

"It's true, but that just shows they all care about her."

"I guess, but we could do without the distraction." He gathered himself together, straightened his shoulders, and ran his fingers through his hair.

It surprised Stella to see a couple of grey hairs in among the jet black. She didn't know exactly how old Jordan was, probably mid-thirties, but he was a good-looking man. His Nana Gloria constantly compared him to Luther, the on-screen detective, but Stella thought Jordan was more handsome. She pushed the thoughts aside. She didn't fancy him. He had a wife and a little boy. But there was nothing wrong with appreciating a fit bloke. The grey was something new, though. Pressure of the job probably. Like the American Presidents who seem to age overnight. "Sorry," she said. "I didn't catch that."

He'd been talking to her. "I asked when you were meeting the Lipscowes' next of kin, the aunty. I'd like to go to Flo's before that if you've time."

Stella looked at her watch. "Yes, should be okay. I'll go in my car and then straight into town. The aunty decided to come through on the train in the end."

Chapter 12

"We're sorry to bother you again," Jordan told Flo. "Some questions have come up and we reckon you're our best bet to find the answers."

"You're alright. I don't mind. Anything I can do to help. Normally, just on Christmas, I'd be run off my feet. Baking and all that stuff. Now, every time I think I'll start something, it hits me again that Trace won't be there. My mind won't settle. I keep wondering how long she'd been lying there, dead. Was she scared, and did she know what was happening?"

"We think she was heavily sedated, so the chances are she just went to sleep and then didn't know anything after that," Stella said.

"I hope so. That's a bit of a comfort. But did Stanley do it? I can tell there's something going on. You wouldn't have all this fuss if she'd just died in her sleep."

"Sorry, Mrs McGrady, we really can't tell you very much. We don't know a lot yet, but it's an ongoing investigation, so we couldn't say much, anyway," Jordan said.

"I can't believe he'd do that. He loved her. They had their bad times like all of us, rows and sulks and stuff. She used to say if he'd upset her. You know, she'd have a whinge, bit of a cry maybe. But they were happy – most of the time, at any rate. Trace being ill put pressure on them, I know that, but they were coping. I thought they were, at any rate. Maybe I was wrong. When will they move the tape and that tent over the door? When will the technicians be done? It's all so upsetting. I asked them if they wanted a drink, but they just asked me to keep away. How can I get over it with all that going on?"

Jordan did his best to reassure her that the scene-of-crime team would be gone as soon as possible. But she must understand they had so much to do, it wasn't possible to know how long they would take. "Best if you just let them get on with it. We'll leave you in peace now. Listen, I know you've already said but you're sure, are you, that Tracy still had carers?"

Flo was insistent that the carers had still been coming. She heard them in the morning and knew someone had arrived.

She couldn't tell them what cars the carers used. "I don't spend my whole time just curtain twitching. There's a loose flagstone, and it gives a really recognisable sound. I'd hear the door go, and that was it. Yes, now I feel guilty, but I did my best. She wasn't my responsibility, was she? That's what the carers are for."

They reassured her she had nothing to feel guilty about, but she didn't look convinced. They left her sitting in front of the gas fire, staring into the fake flames.

"It seems clear she was getting care from somewhere, or someone," Jordan said.

"Bank accounts might give us the information," Stella said. "Listen, I'd better get off to meet the aunty. I'll ask her if she has any clue, but given her reaction up to now, I doubt it."

Jordan slid into his car and checked his phone. The message from Kath was characteristically short. "Something you might like to see. Catch me when you're back in."

Chapter 13

Kath seemed calmer, almost back to being her usual laid-back self. She'd spent the morning reviewing CCTV from the home security system. The images were grainy and black-and-white, but they were backed up on the computer they had taken from the little box room office.

Stanley's car wasn't in front of the house during the night before the motorway incident. It was going to be a bigger job, because they would need to requisition footage from anywhere nearby. Shops, churches, schools, and the council street cameras. They requested all the ones they had identified. Some organisations would be happy to help, others would delay and obfuscate. They would acquire them in the end. They'd done it before, and it was just dogged determination that got results. Right now, Kath focused on the one from the Lipscowes' place.

At the house, there was a lock-up garage. Sergeant Flowers, still at the house managing the scene, was of the opinion that there was no room for a car, not even a mini. Certainly nobody could squeeze in a Vauxhall Astra. The space was filled with cardboard boxes, gardening furniture, rusty tools, and general rubbish. The messy space came in for quite a few derogatory comments about filth and carelessness. When you spend your working life examining other people's property, a craving for order is probably understandable.

"But you said there was something you'd found," Jordan said.

"Yes," said Kath. "It could well turn out to be nothing, but there was a car at the house. It parked in the driveway for a while and then off it went. I know she had carers, so I went back, and there it was, morning and evening for the last few weeks. As far back as the recording goes, anyway. I've noted all the dates and times in the log."

It was confirmation of what the neighbour had said, but Jordan was careful with his reaction. With Kath on a short fuse, he didn't want to risk another episode of tears, but she shook her head at him when he told her what a decent job she was doing. "You need to let me finish, boss."

The car, a Ford Fiesta, was there regularly. They had a few shots of the driver briefly before she went out of range. It was a small woman in what could be a uniform. It looked like a short coat over jeans or trousers. She stayed for varying lengths of time. She used the key safe near the door.

Just confirmation, surely.

There were other vehicles now and then, and Kath had noted in the log that a van was seen often. It parked at the corner and, because of the way the camera had been angled, all that was visible was the bonnet. That was enough to confirm that it was probably white, and to lead them to believe that it was a VW with the snub-nosed front, a T4 or T5. It didn't show the registration nor where the driver went. It was there often enough to be noted, but could be one of so many things. The camera had obviously been a do-it-yourself unit, and the angles were only useful to see part of the front of the house, angled down into the garden.

"I wish people would have their cameras set up professionally," Jordan said.

"I want you to look at this," Kath said, raising her eyebrows and pursing her lips as she presented the *pièce de résistance*.

It was the same car in the same drive. Jordan peered closely at the screen and shook his head. "You'll have to help me out here. Okay, it's raining, it looks cold, and she's got a big coat on. It is the same woman, though."

"Oh God. The time, boss. Look what time it is."

"Oh yes, okay. It's dark for four-thirty, but it's winter. Oh, four-thirty in the morning."

"Hallelujah. Give him a lollipop. Oh, sorry, boss. Sorry. I'm giddy with the painkillers and a bit hyped with everything that's gone on."

Jordan laughed. "It's okay, don't worry. But this is interesting. Why is she visiting in the early hours? Is it just this one time?"

"No. I thought of that. You know, maybe Tracy Lipscowe had a bad night or something, but I went back and she's visited fairly often at around the same time. A bit of leeway, earlier now and again, but always in the middle of the night."

"What about last Monday?"

"No. We couldn't be that lucky, could we? There is no recording for then. The technical department reckon the camera was simply turned off. You can do that with a smartphone from anywhere. Did they find Stanley's phone?"

"Not as far as I'm aware. I will double check." Because of the angle of approach and the camera setting, there were no clear images of the licence plate. They did, though, confirm that it was a small car, very likely a Fiesta. It was dark-coloured and there were a couple of shots of the side of the driver's head as she entered the house.

"I knew you'd get me something," Jordan said. "Listen, if there is anything any of us can do to help, now while you wait, and later when you've had the surgery, don't hesitate, not for a minute."

"Thanks, boss. Everyone has been really kind and I'm calming down about it all now. I'm not the only one in this situation. There's hundreds of us on waiting lists and treatment being delayed and delayed."

"Can you get images of the car, and the best you can manage of that woman, sent to everyone? Don't forget Sergeant Flowers over at the house, just in case it turns up. Unlikely, I suppose, but best to be prepared."

They showed the images to John, who'd been researching care providers, but the uniform wasn't the same as the lilac tabard the original care company used. It went some way to confirm the change, and they left him trawling the internet again to find a company whose workers dressed in something similar.

Chapter 14

It was after shift change when Stella arrived in the office. She brought a take-away carton of fish and chips. The smell of hot fat and vinegar caused groans from all across the room. It wasn't long before John was in his car and heading for the chippy with a list of requests.

"I thought everyone would have gone by now," Stella said. "I would have eaten them in the car otherwise."

"Don't worry, we should probably all have something. The CCTV has everyone focused, but it's not good to go on and on. It leads to mistakes," Jordan said.

While they waited for the food to arrive, Jordan brought Stella up to date. She stood in front of the whiteboard, chewing chips, and studying the grainy images from the security camera.

"I know this isn't the same care company, but it might be worth asking the original one if they ever had to send someone in the night," she said.

"Yeah, John was on that, before he pulled the chippy run duty," Jordan said, grinning.

"Oops. My bad. Do you want me to do it?"

"No, he's got a bit of rapport going with the manager. You could lend a hand looking for other companies with a similar uniform. That's the place to start, anyway. If we don't find one, then we have to call all the care providers and ask them if they were servicing the Lipscowes' address."

"Not much to go on with the angle and everything, but I'll give it a go. Why don't I call the council and ask them if they know?"

But it was too late. The offices were closed. Instead, they sat at Stella's desk while she told him about the strange meeting with Gwynne Porter, Tracy's aunt.

Stella had thought that perhaps the true situation hadn't registered with the woman. She had expected that when they entered the low, brick building, and experienced the smell and the sounds of the morgue and then the reveal of the body, she may fall apart. Stella was ready for it. There was a pack of tissues in her pocket and she had sussed out the nearest place to go for a restorative cuppa. What she wasn't ready for was the casual glance at both bodies and the quiet but definite, "Yes, that's Tracy, my niece. Lipscowe, Flynne as was." Then the broken body of her nephew-in-law. She wrinkled her nose as they uncovered his battered face. "God, he's a bit bashed about, isn't he?" But she confirmed Stanley's identity. There were no tears, no emotion. As they left, she asked for directions to somewhere she could have a bite to eat. "Not a pub, though," she'd said with a sniff.

Stella directed her to Liverpool One which had a wide choice of cafés and restaurants.

"That was it?" Jordan asked.

"Pretty much. She just didn't seem bothered. I got a bit of information from her when I picked her up at Lime Street. She hadn't seen either of them for ages. They weren't close – well, that was really obvious from her behaviour. She was concerned about funeral arrangements, but that was it. One thing was odd. Although really the whole thing was peculiar," Stella said. "In her opinion, it was probably a good thing that Tracy had gone now before she got any worse. Also, it was best Stanley wasn't left on his own because he was a weak man, and wouldn't have coped without a woman around. I don't think she liked him very much. She was cold and dismissive, and I don't think we'll get anything of any value from her," Stella said. "You expect family to be close, I suppose, if your own is. I just thought this was sad."

There wasn't much more that could be done.

"Fancy a bevvy before we get off home?" John said.

"Just a quick one," said Jordan. "I've missed Harry's bedtime already and Penny's got her sister round. They're wrapping presents. They won't miss me."

"It's hard to get into the mood now, isn't it? I guess there's not much chance of us getting off for the holidays," John said.

"I'll see what I can arrange, John. Tell you what, let's get a list together of people who have definite arrangements and see what we can do."

Chapter 15

The pub was lively. Some local firms had already worked their last day before the break and there were paper hats, and crackers, and loud voices. Jordan, Stella, and John sat at a table in the corner and watched it going on around them. Stella said, "If you make a list, boss, I want to work if possible. Right now, I'm not in the mood for drunken arguments and scryking kids. It would have been impossible for me to get out of it without an excuse and with respect to Stanley, he could rescue me."

* * *

Jordan was almost home when his phone chimed. He could have let it go to messaging but Ted Bliss, the crime scene manager, wouldn't ring so late unless it was urgent. He pressed the phone button on his steering wheel.

The first part of the conversation was an irritated rant about timing and consideration and inconvenience. He wanted to know how come they were only just getting pictures of a visitor to the scene now. He sounded tired and frustrated rather than angry, and Jordan let him have his say.

By the time the list of complaints was over, he had parked in his drive. The warm house, hot chocolate, and a welcoming wife were just steps away. "We've only just been able to access those. I had them sent across as soon as possible. I thought you could include them in the house-to-house tomorrow. You haven't finished that yet, have you?"

"Well, it's fine that tomorrow is soon enough for some people," Bliss said. "Good job we're not all so laid back. I had my guys out revisiting houses as soon as we had those images."

"What can I say, Ted? Thank you." Jordan slid across the seat and clicked open his car door as quietly as he could. "I didn't expect you to get onto it so quickly."

"Well…" The word was quieter, and it was obvious Bliss' short temper was calming. "We had to go back to some, anyway. People were out at work the first time round and what have you. Anyway, I wouldn't have bothered you as you have obviously clocked off for the day" – another sly barb – "but this witness is off on holiday tomorrow. Leaving from John Lennon Airport for Alicante, and won't be back for two weeks. Best to have a word now, I reckon. It could be interesting and well worth your while. Reckons he saw your motorway victim on Monday morning."

Jordan swung his legs round, pulled the door closed and reversed out of the drive as Penny opened the front door. He waved to her, blew a kiss and wagged his phone at the window, letting her know he'd call her.

She shook her head and raised her hands in a 'what the hell' gesture, before turning back and pushing the door closed.

"Give me the address, Ted. I'm on my way. Will I see you there?"

"No, you bloody won't. Me and my lot are off down the pub. We've put in a long day. Good luck with Tony Yates." With that, he hung up.

It started to rain.

Chapter 16

Many of the houses were decorated with festive lights, illuminated now in the rain-speckled darkness. There were dangling Santas, some of which were already deflating, and unlikely wire reindeer standing on soggy lawns or gravel parking spaces. The potholes and gutters ran with grubby water but the reflected light sparkled and flashed in the puddles. It was a sort of magic and after the recent Covid Christmases Jordan understood the need for over-the-top celebration. Penny had put a few things around the house to amuse Harry, but the plan had been to travel down to see the family. Nana Gloria and Jordan's mum would have everywhere looking like a fairground, and there would be more food than anyone could eat. He had kept things professional in the office, stating the facts baldly, but he was as brassed off as John and the others. It would hurt missing Christmas with the family.

He wondered briefly what Stella's problem was. She was close to her relatives and enjoyed get-togethers. She always had done before, anyway. Surely it wasn't the case that was getting to her. He should make time to have a word.

Tony Yates lived opposite the corner house that had been home to Stanley and Tracy Lipscowe. It had a decent view of the front garden and the road outside. There was no security camera. Ted Bliss would already have checked the area, but Jordan couldn't help scanning the neighbours' places.

The door swung open quickly in response to the bell. Tony was a big man with a shaved head. He had a dark, bushy beard, and his blue T-shirt revealed a sleeve tattoo over his right arm. He was imposing and could have been intimidating, but he smiled and held out a friendly hand as Jordan flashed his warrant card.

There was a black travel bag in the hall with a puffa jacket laid across the top. He would look enormous wearing the padded coat. Maybe not the person you would choose to sit next to on a flight.

"Do ya want a bevvy, mate?" Tony picked up a can of lager and waved it towards Jordan.

"Thanks, best not. I had a drink earlier and I have to drive. Technically, I'm on duty as well."

"Aye, but, you know, it's Crimbo."

"True enough, but I won't. I hope not to keep you long. You've probably got stuff to do."

"I'm pretty well sorted. It doesn't take me long to pack."

"Are you going on your own?"

"I'm meeting mates there."

"Just men?"

"Aye, lads' trip to Spain. My wife did a bunk a couple of years ago and I can't face this place" – he waved a hand around – "on my own at Christmas. So, some of us who are not in relationships meet up. We don't do much traditional stuff. We have a villa, play video games, snooker and whatnot and try to zone out from the hoo-ha."

"Fair enough. Sorry about your wife."

"Thanks. It was great at first and sometimes I miss her, but by the time she went we were miserable more often than we were happy. Calling it a bust was the best thing. No kids, so it was a clean break. Sad, she stuck by me all the time I was in the army and it fell apart when I came home. Shouldn't be that way, should it?"

"No. What is it you do now?"

"A bit of this, a bit of that – you know how it is. There's always somebody wanting a hand with something. Decorating, gardening. A bit of nightclub security, but just casual."

"Right. My scene manager says you saw Stanley Lipscowe on Monday morning."

"Yes. I don't sleep that well, so I get up and watch telly, have a cuppa, whatever. There's not much goes on round here at night, but I saw the lights when the car turned out of their garden. I got up to have a look, and it was just off down the road. Hey, is it true they've both snuffed it? I know she was sick, but I didn't think there was owt wrong with him."

"Sorry, I can't tell you much, but yes, unfortunately, they have both died."

"What was it, a car crash?"

"No."

"Only we leave at about the same time most days. So it was odd, him going so early."

"What time was all this?"

"I can't say exactly, early hours. I stood there for a good long while. Went back up just before five. It's a bugger not sleeping."

"That's really useful. Are you leaving early tomorrow?"

"Earlyish, but if you need to speak to me again, I can give you my phone number."

"Great."

He handed over his mobile phone and, as Jordan entered the number, he asked, "What's your next move, then?"

"Sorry, I really can't discuss it."

"Fair enough, but I mean, are we in danger or anything?"

It was such an odd question from this big man who had no woman or child to protect. Jordan pursed his lips and shook his head. "No reason to think so. Of course, if that were to change, we'd be sure to let everyone know. When are you back?"

"Oh, not really sure. It'll depend on the weather and how long my mates can stay."

They shook hands again, wished each other a merry Christmas and Jordan left Tony Yates to his solitary drinking and his tin of toffees.

Chapter 17

Back at the station, Jordan noted on the whiteboard about the car, "John, any luck tracing that uniform?" he said.

"Sorry, boss. Nothing. I reckon me and Stel have looked at every care company on Merseyside and we haven't found anything like it. A lot of them just use their own clothes and wear tabards over the top. I'm going to carry on today just cold-calling care companies. I made a start last night but it'll take forever. Mostly, it's the usual data protection stuff, nobody wants to say anything about anything just in case they screw up. Nine times out of ten they pass the buck and I have to ring back to speak to someone else and then the head office and, Jesus, it goes on and on."

"I know. We've got some information about a car leaving early now, though," said Jordan.

"Yay."

Kath spoke up. "Who gave you that, boss?"

"The neighbour opposite. He saw the lights, apparently. He reckons it was Stanley leaving early."

"Oh, right."

"What?"

"Nothing, really. I didn't think it was an Astra. Could be because he was seeing it at night. If you just see the headlights, you'd need to be very knowledgeable to know. I'll do a comparison."

"Okay. Go for it. He could just be mistaken."

Kath grinned at him. "Yeah, I guess that's it, boss."

"Stella, you could contact the aunt today. If she's up for it, we can organise an interim death certificate so she can move things forward with funeral arrangements. Also, have we had anything else from the house-to-house enquiries?"

"Not yet. There are still a couple more addresses. As for the aunt, I don't think she wants to know, boss. She said, and I quote, 'I hope it's not going to be down to me to see them off.'"

"Nice. Okay. Let her know and if she's not interested, we'll see what the other options are. There's no other family."

"Maybe the neighbour," Stella said.

"It's a big ask. Anyway, we can hand it over to the local authority and they can sort it. Speak to the aunt, just out of respect. She might have changed her mind."

"There is one bright spot, boss," Stella said. "They've found Tracy's phone. The battery was flat, and it'd had slid under the bedside cabinet. They charged it up and there are messages to and from Stanley. The technical department is sending us a copy of the last three weeks as a start."

"Brilliant. That's more like it. Soon as we get that, go through it. Keep me updated."

"Ted Bliss said they should be out of the house tomorrow, but up to now they haven't really found anything startling," Stella said.

"One step at a time, guys. We'll sort this. Okay, I need a list of whoever has firm plans for the next week and we'll do what we can to allow leave."

There was a muffled cheer, mostly from the civilian clerks. Jordan hoped he hadn't spoken too soon.

Chapter 18

Jordan spent the next couple of hours catching up on paperwork and reviewing the murder book for Tracy Lipscowe. The account of the discovery of her body was easy. He'd been there. There were notes about the neighbour, the aunt, and the cause of death. There had to be a mention of her illness and references made to the doctor's comments. Then there was Stanley. This could be a neat way to tidy it all up and put it to bed quickly. He doubted there would be many naysayers. What they had so far would probably convince the coroner. The most likely scenario was that Stanley had killed his wife out of a sense of compassion, maybe frustration, or simply exhaustion and despair. It was the conclusion the DCI had reached already. When they'd scraped his remains off the carriageway just a few short days ago, everyone accepted that he had committed suicide. There would be no expensive trial and they could record it as a clear up.

The last message from DCI Josh Lewis had been to stop looking for complications, draw a line and let the team have their Christmas break.

And yet. There were things unexplained, and that didn't sit well with Jordan.

He closed the book and walked over to where Stella was printing out copies of text messages.

"This has just come in, boss. I thought if I printed it out, I could go down to the canteen and review it over a cuppa and a butty."

"Good idea. I'll come with you if you like. I can do some. Shouldn't take long."

"Ace. I'll treat you to a mince pie."

The canteen was quiet between shift changes. Jordan ordered a chicken pie. He knew it was chicken because the label said so. It had some bits of carrot and some peas in there and a sort of gluey white gravy. The flavour had been lost somewhere along the way. He had one in the freezer at home, his mum's recipe. This was a distant relative of that, to be sure. He glanced at Stella's tuna sandwich and wished he'd gone that way. The mince pies were lovely, though. Crispy pastry, plenty of filling and just warm enough. So, altogether not a total bust.

The pages of text held his attention. He highlighted lines as he moved his finger down the paper. Eventually, he looked up to find that Stella was frowning into her coffee cup as she finished the last crumbs of pastry.

"The neighbour, Flo, said they were happy, didn't she?" Stella said. "The odd row and the problems with her health, but generally getting along."

"Yes, and his boss gave the impression of someone who cared about his wife and worried about her."

"So" – Stella picked up her sheet of paper and wagged it in the air – "I'm wondering if you have the same impression as I do?"

"Let's swap," Jordan said.

They slid the printouts across the table and there were a few quiet minutes as they read again.

Jordan was the first to speak. "These don't read to me like a happily married couple. Flo told me Tracy would share now and again when there was friction, but she can't have shared this, can she?"

"Snarling at each other." Stella pointed to the papers. "Swearing there, she's calling him some interesting names. If they really used to be happy together, they weren't any more. Not at the time she died, anyway. I guess that backs up the idea that he killed her."

"Does it? If so, why did he then spread himself all over the motorway? Wouldn't he just be glad to be rid? She really was laying into him."

"Still, guilt, or maybe even fear when he realised what he'd done."

"Yes, I get that," said Jordan. "There's something else, though. I don't think there's any doubt that Tracy thought he'd been unfaithful."

"But she says she understands, even though she can't forgive him. This is heavy going for just a few weeks. As though things suddenly went haywire."

"We need to have whatever else the digital forensics can get from it. Back as far as possible."

"He did it, though, didn't he?" asked Stella. "I mean, she'd turned into a harridan."

"But look at the ones from the days before he died. He's trying to mend fences. He's begging her to be patient, and then in the one from the day before, he says to let him sort it and they can make a new start. We know he wasn't at work for a couple of days. Where was he and what was he doing?" Jordan said.

"If he killed her and then topped himself, I guess he did. Sort it, I mean."

Jordan blew out his cheeks and shrugged. "This has just left me with more questions. It's brilliant that we have it. We were bloody lucky there, but I don't feel that it's answered all my doubts."

"If that's your gut feeling, boss, we'll just have to keep going."

"That won't make John happy, will it?" He thought this might be an opportunity to find out whether there was anything on Stella's mind.

"You want to work, though?" Jordan said.

"Oh, that. Yeah." She paused, and Jordan was surprised to see her eyes mist with tears for a moment. She brushed them aside. "Don't take any notice. I'm just a daft mare."

51

"What's the problem? We're mates, you know that. If you want to talk, I'm here."

Chapter 19

Jordan gave Stella a minute to compose herself. "I'll get another cuppa. Do you want one?"

She nodded.

By the time he brought the drinks to the table, she had gathered the papers into a pile and pushed away the dirty plates. She had her hands folded on the Formica top.

"It's all okay," she said, as she took the cup. "I'm being high-maintenance, a daft bitch. You should take no notice."

Jordan shook his head. "Not you. Never."

She sipped her coffee. "You know all about the money and my worries about it, don't you?"

She was referring to the lottery win that had happened early in their first case together. Jordan knew she had been hesitant to even accept the money at first. Then when she did, she made all efforts to keep it secret. Her fear was that if colleagues and friends found out, they would treat her differently. She loved her job and never considered leaving the force. It wasn't tens of millions, but it was enough that she would never have to worry about money. A fair proportion of the funds had been spent on her family, to buy them houses, to pay for her granddad's hip replacement. She had bought the converted house where her flat was and had it refurbished. A new car had replaced an old unreliable banger. She was happy with the choices she'd made.

"I tried hard not to let it make a difference. I thought I'd got it right. Some people asked if they could have a lend of some. I gave them what they needed. I told 'em to pay me back if they could, but not to worry. Some have, some haven't. A couple tried to tap me for money for holidays or to buy new tellies. I stood firm. I mean, that's not a good way to go. You shouldn't borrow for things you could save for. That's my feeling, anyway."

Jordan nodded and listened in silence.

"Geoff, my mum's brother—" She paused and rubbed a hand over her face. "We got on okay, didn't see him a lot when I was a kid. He used to go to the match with Granda sometimes, just part of the family, nan's favourite, I reckon. He turned up at weddings and what have you. Got divorced a few years ago. There're a couple of kids. Grown up now, of course. We used to play together. Anyway, he's a builder. He's okay at it, I think, but nothing special. A while ago he comes to me to ask for money to buy some land and for me to fund a development of houses. He was full of it. It was going to be brilliant, make us both a fortune, the start of him going big. A bit late, given he's in his fifties, nearly sixty probably. I wasn't interested. I squirreled away the money I have left, so if anything happens with the job or whatever, I'll be okay. But, more than that, I can't be doing with the hassle. He says he'll do all the business stuff, hire workers and whatnot. But it's going to be one big pain in the arse. Even worse, he wants to go into business with his mate and, to put it bluntly, I can't stand that bloke. I don't think he's kosher. I don't trust him and can't be around him."

"And he's going to be at your mum's for Christmas," Jordan said.

She nodded. "Now he's on his own, the kids are both living away and are going to their mother's, so Mam's asked him round. I know I should tell him to bog off, but he's always on, every chance he gets, and I just can't be arsed. It'll end in disaster and now I'm uncomfortable to be around my own family. I knew this would happen, didn't I? I knew that bloody money would bring trouble."

She rubbed a finger end under her eye. "I thought I could go to Mam's on Christmas Eve, help her with the cooking and have a bevvy with them and then use this job as an excuse not to rock up on Sunday. Mam'll sulk a bit, but she can't say much if I tell her it's work."

Chapter 20

Jordan held out a thin paper tissue, and Stella dabbed at her eyes and nose.

She spat out an expletive. "I'm better than this. I'm not a bloody wimp. What is the matter with me?"

Hiding at work, avoiding her uncle, was pointless because he was going to be there until she solved the problem. She wasn't going into any sort of business with him. Never. She wasn't lending him money to give to his dodgy mate. But just saying no over and over wasn't going to cut it. She had to stop the constant hassle, the phone calls, and the unexpected visits.

"How bent is the mate, do you know?" Jordan said.

"He did time. It was just when we all left school. I remember there was a lot of whispering in the house and Uncle Geoff hanging around for a few days drinking beer and smoking. Everybody looked worried, but in the end, nothing happened to Geoff. The rumour was that his mate had been dealing, but I don't know, exactly. Later, he was involved with a car sales place that closed down suddenly and was left empty for ages. The cars sat out front for weeks. Kids vandalized them and eventually, inevitably I suppose, it all went up in flames. Carl Reynolds vanished for a bit, but now he's back like a bad penny. There was talk that one of his girlfriends had a restraining order issued. Seems to be a genuine bad lot, but Geoff has known him since they were kids. He won't accept that he's a no-mark and a scally. He just says he made bad choices and was unlucky. Sometimes, I think Geoff must be one sandwich short of a picnic."

"Have you looked on HOLMES and the PNC?" Jordan asked.

She hadn't and knew that by now she really should have done. "It's Granda. Whenever I think of fronting up to Geoff, all I can see are his eyes looking mournful."

"They'll be more than mournful if you and your uncle get involved with this bloke. You know that." He told her to take the rest of the afternoon to do her research. Once she had enough evidence, then she could show her uncle that his mate was dodgy, she didn't trust him and wasn't happy to be involved. She'd also tell Geoff he'd be best advised to keep away. "Just tell him to do one," Jordan said.

"Did you really just say that? 'Tell him to do one.' You're down with the kids you are, boss. You'll be wearing trabs and a beanie next."

Jordan grinned as he left her scrolling through HOLMES records and logged on to his own machine. There was a preliminary report from the SOC sergeant.

The Lipscowes' house was a stew of forensic evidence. Dozens of different fingerprints and physical evidence. A feast of DNA. That was not a good thing. It would take weeks to analyse everything and unless someone was already on the database, it would be next to useless, anyway. Much of it was probably the result of Tracy being ill. When she was well, chances were that the cleaning would be more thorough. There wouldn't have been so many strangers wandering around the bedrooms and bathrooms. Jordan made a note to find out if there had been a cleaner employed or whether the couple were managing the housekeeping themselves. Flo might know.

He phoned Ted Bliss to arrange for one of the house-to-house officers to have a word with her.

"Too late, chum," Bliss told him. "We're finished, just about. Most of my lads have gone back to the office. Not much to report. I'll send the records through, but nobody knew nothing. Nobody saw nothing and anyway, don't we know it's Christmas? That's about the gist of it. There's one house that we haven't been able to get an answer from. The bloke's an old fella apparently, and he just won't answer the door. We've seen him sitting in a chair by the window, but he just shakes his fist at us. I don't think it's worth worrying about it too much. Although he has a good view of the house."

"Tell you what, I'll call in. I need to speak to Mrs McGrady. Perhaps the uniforms were freaking him out." He winced. He really had to cut back on the slang.

"Up to you, but probably more trouble than it's worth. I'll see you in the morning at the drinks thing with DCI Lewis – such fun that'll be. Cheap wine and a sausage roll. I'd rather he just got us a pizza in and left us be." Bliss grinned a bit sheepishly. "Okay, pretend I didn't say that."

Chapter 21

John drove a pool car out to the Lipscowes' house. The heater didn't work and there was a leak in the passenger-side window. Jordan's seat was damp and cold. He thought they used to maintain them better and said so.

"Money, I reckon, cutting back on staff."

"If they're trying to get us to use our own cars, it's going to work." Jordan reached into the rear seat where someone had left a high-viz jacket and slid it under his bum.

"Not this time," John said. "My car's in dock with some sort of ignition problem, according to the mechanic.

Won't be out now until after the holiday. So, that's me stuck with these bloody things."

A cold driving rain forced their heads down as they parked in the gravelled frontage of the crime-scene house. The tent over the door had gone, and the tape had been removed from the fence. Jordan hoped it would please Flo McGrady and help her put memories of the last few days to rest.

When she answered the knock on the door, she was wearing a smart, blue dress with a paler cardigan over the top. She had on a pair of earrings shaped like Christmas trees, her hair was styled and her face made up.

"Sorry, are you going out?" Jordan said. "We won't keep you. It's just a quick question."

She ushered them in out of the rain and showed them through to her living room. There were more presents under the tree than before and a bowl of nuts on the sideboard. She insisted they have a drink, offering them beer and wine. In the end, Jordan accepted a glass of sherry, but John insisted that driving the police car he couldn't risk anything and finally agreed to a glass of pop.

The Lipscowes had employed a cleaner, a local woman who had worked for them for over a year. Flo hadn't seen her arriving recently and agreed that the house had been deteriorating. "Perhaps they couldn't afford her anymore. Though I don't reckon she can charge that much. She's only local, not from a company or anything, I don't think. Mind you, I don't know. I wouldn't have someone cleaning my place. Wouldn't suit me at all. Then Tracy was in a different situation." She couldn't remember the woman's name, but knew she lived near the Catholic school. She glanced at the clock several times.

"We won't keep you. You look very nice. Are you off out?" Jordan said.

She blushed and fingered the frill around the top of her dress.

"It's just a get-together with the ladies I go line dancing with. It'll be fun. I thought it'd take my mind off things. Tracy would have been coming. She didn't dance, of course, but she enjoyed the music and the company."

As they made ready to leave, Jordan asked about the old man in the house opposite.

A local character, Flo explained, the sort of old bloke who yelled at children if they went into his garden, and shouted at canvassers at election time. He had lived in the house for as long as anyone could remember. There had been a wife at one time, but she'd died years ago.

"It looks well kept, for an older person's place," Jordan said.

"Oh, aye. He used to have it painted every couple of years. Not so much recently, though. Don't know what it might be like inside, mind you. I don't envy you wanting to talk to him," Flo said. She hitched a shoulder towards the house next to hers as they left. "Is it all done there now?"

"For the moment, yes. I don't know whether we've completely finished, but at least we can leave it alone, probably until the new year."

"Right, that's good. What'll happen then?"

Jordan shook his head. "Probably just go to the next of kin and she'll put it up for sale."

"I don't know why anyone would want to buy it, given what happened there. Are you any nearer to knowing just what went on?"

Jordan knew that any information he gave now would be the source of most of the gossip between the dancing and the snacking. He shrugged and shook his head. "Ongoing, for the moment. Can't really discuss it."

Flo hid her disappointment well as she wished them a merry Christmas and pushed her door closed against the rain.

Chapter 22

Heavy green curtains shifted as John and Jordan walked up the short path. Lights inside were turned on against the afternoon gloom. There were no seasonal decorations here. No gnomes, no fairy lights, or plastic holly wreath. The garden was a simple square of lawn. One rose bush in the centre was pruned for the winter.

Jordan rattled the lid of the letter box in the absence of bell or knocker. He avoided hammering on the wood with his fist. No matter how taciturn, this was an older person on his own and he didn't want to cause alarm.

There was no response, although the curtain moved again. They saw a hand gripping the edge and as they watched, two fingers raised in an unmistakable gesture. Jordan grinned.

Jordan moved across the path. "Sorry to bother you. I'm DI Carr with my colleague, DC Grice. We really could do with a word. There's been a couple of incidents concerning the people in the house opposite and we have questions. You're not obliged to speak to us, but we would be grateful."

John had taken his wallet from his pocket and pulled out a photograph. He held it up to the window. "This is Bella. She's ten years old now. How old was Sherpa?"

The curtain shifted and the old man's face came nearer to the glass. He waved his hand in a 'come nearer' gesture. John stretched out his hand and pressed the print against the window.

"We had another before him. A border collie cross, Trudy; she was brilliant. Had her all the time I was growing up." John fished out another picture and held it out.

The curtains fell back into place and after a few minutes they heard the locks on the front door rattle.

"I had a border collie. Brilliant bitch, she was. Cancer got her in the end." The old man said, and with that, they were in. Frank Dirkin held out his hand, and John gave him the picture of his dog. Frank nodded, handed it back, and then stood aside. John walked in first, Jordan followed, and the old man took them into his living room.

The room was tidy. An old-fashioned three-piece suite was arranged in front of a gas fire. There was central heating but, when Jordan brushed his hand across the radiator, he felt no warmth. On the mantlepiece there was a framed wedding picture and three smaller frames with images of dogs in them. Frank picked up the nearest one. "That's Sherpa. I lost him two years ago now. Still not over it. The other two are Casper and Floyd. They're long gone. Casper was my wife's dog, really. Ha, she's long gone as well." He touched the wedding picture with a fingertip.

"I can't offer you a drink. I know it's Christmas, but I don't have anything in just now."

"That's okay," Jordan said. "Could I trouble you for a glass of water, though?"

"Aye, no trouble. Can you get it yourself? My arthritis is giving me gip this affie."

The kitchen was clean. It didn't look as though anyone had updated it since the house was new, but the cabinets were in good condition. Jordan opened a cupboard door to find a glass. He looked in the fridge. Inside, there was a pint of milk in a glass bottle. A tin of baked beans, already opened, and a half pack of streaky bacon.

Back in the living room, John was asking all the questions.

Had he known the Lipscowes?

Not well, but his wife got on alright with Tracy.

Had he noticed the carers arriving?

He had. They had a uniform a bit like a nurse's, one he'd seen in other places around the estate. Everyone seemed to need some help these days. "We're all getting older," said Frank. "We could do with some fresh blood around here, otherwise it's like we're all just waiting to see who falls off the twig next. I reckon it'll be me soon."

There was no point gainsaying the comment. Frank Dirkin looked tired. His skin was dry, and his eyes looked sore. Where muscles on his arms had wasted away, the flesh hung slack, and his trousers bagged on skinny legs.

Jordan asked, "Did you ever see a vehicle arrive very late at night? Maybe if you couldn't sleep or got up for a drink sometime."

"You know, don't you, son? Us oldies, we don't sleep. So, we get up and watch the box, maybe we read. My wife used to read. I never could be doing with it much. I did used to take Sherpa for a walk. Didn't matter what time it was, me and him roamed round the streets in the quiet. It were nice. My Gladys didn't like it, she said it weren't safe. Anyway, not now. I don't have Sherpa. So, yes, I sit there by the window, and I watch. Not much to see. In that London, they say they see foxes. I never saw no fox. A cat now and then, sometimes a drunk wobbling home." He gave a rattly laugh.

"And the house across the road?" Jordan said.

"Oh, aye. Some car coming in the early hours of the morning. The lights on upstairs, then the car going off again. No prizes for guessing what went on there. Not that I'm judging anyone. Each to his own, I reckon. She were sick, that Tracy, and he isn't an old man, if you get my drift. I saw they took her away the other day. Poor lass. He hasn't been back since. Surely he didn't go off and leave her?"

"Are you sure it was a car?"

"How'd'ya mean am I sure? It weren't a camel."

Jordan laughed. "Sorry, what I mean is, could it have been a van or a people carrier, something like that?"

"I can tell the difference. If it were a van, I'd have said it were a van, wouldn't I? It were a car, like I say it were a little car, a girl's car. Though now you mention it…"

"Yes."

"Though… wait a bit, Monday, you're talking about. It were a van then. Yes, the car early on and then later. I only saw it driving away from the corner, mind you. I were in the toilet, ha, when am I not? So, I can't say for certain it came from there, but it seemed like it."

"And this was definitely Monday?"

The old man pulled at his lower lip. He frowned. "When you're my age and on your own, all the days drift into one. I don't have weekends anymore, not as such. If I were to be forced, I would say yes. Saturday was noisy. One of the houses had a party, and they were shouting a bit and singing. Wasn't that bad, but it were definitely Saturday and the car wasn't there when I was looking out. So, if I had to put money on it, not that I've got any, I'd say yes, Monday. Don't ask me what time exactly because I don't look at the clock. No point counting the hours when they're all the same."

"Thanks for all that. It's really useful. I'm sorry to have to tell you, Stanley Lipscowe is dead, Frank. He was killed on the motorway last Monday."

"Aw, shit. S'cuse my French. Bloody motorways. Everyone driving too fast. That'll be coming up for sale now, I suppose. I hope we get a young family in. Kids are a bloody pain in the arse, but you need 'em around the place to make it feel alive."

They talked for a while longer. Jordan gave Frank a card with his mobile number on the back. "If you need any help any time, mate, just give me a ring."

"Don't expect I'll be needing police. Never have before."

The curtains twitched again as they walked down the path, heads lowered against the driving rain. In the car, Jordan asked John, "How did you know?"

"What's that, boss?"

"How did you know about the dog?"

"Under the rose tree. A slate with his name on and a little picture etched on it. We got one for our Trudy, for where we put her in the back garden. Dogs, they're part of the family. You never had one, boss?"

"No. I've thought about it, but maybe when Harry is older."

"Yeah. A boy needs a dog, I reckon."

Chapter 23

It was late. When they arrived in Copy Lane, John took the pool car home and Jordan went up to the office to collect his laptop and briefcase. He scanned the messages. There was one from the forensic laboratory. It was interim, sent through because they were cutting back on staff for the next few days, until the week before New Year's Day. Vickie Frost, the SOCO sergeant, had festooned the email heading with a sleigh and reindeer. There had been an incredible amount to go through in the house, but this was a report on the clothes and belongings from the scene on the motorway. She had highlighted a section relating to Stanley's underwear. There was evidence that he had urinated. Not surprising, given what he was about to do, but the stain had soaked through to his outer clothes. She had added a comment that, in her opinion, this must have happened quite a while before he jumped. Surely it was understandable, given he knew what he was planning. There was something about it that had caused her to mention it. Jordan frowned as he read the comment. The clothes were torn, dirty, and blood soaked, none of which was a surprise. She singled out the urine stain, though. There was an asterisk, which linked to another part of the document.

The SOC technicians examined the car. They had pulled it apart, and still had work to do. Again, there was a huge amount of evidence. The hairs and skin flakes, the fingernails – Jordan highlighted this – the fabric threads. They had sent away everything of note and results would come back probably in the new year. They expected there would be DNA from some of it, particularly the fingernail. The next part had been highlighted. Urine residue was found. It was not on the driver's seat. The carpet in the car's boot was stained. This is where they had found the fingernail, along with a small amount of blood. Jordan stared at the report as his mind went into overdrive. His stomach clenched…

It was conceivable that Stanley might sit in the rear seats, maybe the passenger seat, to think through what was happening. But there could only be one reason for him to be in the boot.

Jordan examined the picture of the small space. He picked up his phone and called Stella. "Can you look at the report from Vickie Frost and ring me later?"

He gathered up his belongings and left the office. It was past the rush hour and he was home in just over twenty minutes. Penny had parked her car at the roadside. He remembered she was leaving early in the morning. She would need her car to be at the end of the drive nearest to the gate. He sighed. This was not the Christmas he'd been hoping for. Harry was nearly three, old enough now to pick up on the excitement, even if he didn't fully understand all of it. Missing his face on Christmas morning as he opened his presents with his extended family around him was a precious moment that would come once, just like this. Jordan loved his job, but sometimes it broke his heart.

There were bags and parcels in the hallway. Harry ran to meet him and, as he bent to pick him up, Jordan had to fight to keep the emotion under control.

Penny appeared in the kitchen doorway with a glass of wine for him. She had cooked a salmon en croute. It had been their traditional Christmas Eve meal every year since they met, and when she had been low with postnatal depression, he had cooked it for her.

He threw his son into the air to make him giggle and kissed his wife. There was no way around it. This was probably the most he was going to get of Christmas, given the implications of the report from the laboratory. There was no point spoiling it, wishing it was different. He raised the wine in a toast and kicked off his shoes.

Chapter 24

The light sneaking in through the gap in the curtains was grey and dim. Jordan heard his son running up and down the landing and Penny shushing him, telling him not to disturb Daddy. He lay quietly for a while, just listening until the door creaked slowly open and Harry's face appeared in the gap.

"He's up, Mummy, he's up. Can I go in?"

Jordan laughed and threw back the bedding so his little boy could squirm in beside him. It was bittersweet. They were leaving for the trip to London, and he should have been up and packing his own stuff in the car to go with them.

As they drove away, Harry was waving both arms and laughing. Penny had sighed as Jordan promised if there was the slightest possibility he could join them, then he would. She knew already it was a forlorn hope.

After he'd pulled his suit out of the wardrobe, he remembered the drinks meeting with DCI Lewis. Did that mean uniform? He took it out of the cupboard and looked at it for a minute. It wasn't that he minded putting it on. For a long time, he'd worn one like it, with fewer bits of bling. But it meant that he'd have to change in work. He couldn't do the things he needed to unless he was in plain clothes.

If Lewis didn't like it, then he'd leave the reception. It was a waste of time he didn't have, anyway. He was giving up his Christmas with the family, but not so that he could stand around chinwagging and drinking.

After a quick root around in the fridge and freezer, with a piece of toast in his hand and coffee in his go-cup, he left.

Stella was already in the office when he arrived. She looked the same as always. Business smart, but she had eschewed the uniform as well. She was in front of her computer with a notebook open on the desk.

"All okay, Stel?"

"I guess so. I've been researching the bloke my uncle is mixed up with and it's horrible. It's no surprise, I knew he was a lowlife, but once I started, one thing led to another and it's worse than I thought. No way can I let Uncle Geoff go into business with him. I can't believe he doesn't know. Christ, I hope he doesn't know. If he does, then I have to wonder about Geoff, and if I go that route, I could break my granda's heart."

"But Geoff knows you're on the job. Surely he wouldn't be stupid enough to get you involved in something dodgy."

"He's a chancer and the sort of pillock who thinks women are thick. He's still not sure we should be allowed to drive. I reckon he's hoping I'll go into something blind if he offers me the opportunity to make money. He would at the drop of a hat. Can we talk about it in depth some time? I'm hoping I'll be able to put a stop to this before he gets in over his head."

"Absolutely. I'm on my own at home now. Why don't you come round to mine, and we'll have something to eat? I've got a curry in the freezer."

"Yes, please."

"I just have a stop to make on the way home. It won't take long. I suppose we should get off to this reception thing. Have you seen John? I need to know where he's up to with the Lipscowes' bank accounts."

"He was here earlier but I reckon he's gone to get some proper breakfast in case the stuff in the DCI's office is too fancy for him. A quiche is highfalutin as far as John's concerned. A bacon butty and builder's tea is his idea of breakfast and, as for Bucks Fizz, forget it."

It wasn't as bad or as long as they had feared, and there were hot sausage rolls that went down well, even with John, who was seen giving the quiche the side eye. But it wasn't what Jordan wanted them doing. They had a murderer to catch. He hadn't spoken to the team about the report from the lab. He tried to get the DCI on his own, but it was impossible. In the end, he slipped away and sent him an email to let him know that, as far as he was concerned, Stanley Lipscowe was kidnapped and murdered, and this cast serious doubt on who had been involved in the death of Tracy.

He updated his murder book for the wife and opened another for Stanley. Next, he contacted the vehicle pound and told them he'd be coming down later to see the car himself. There followed a long chat on the phone with Vickie in the lab, who agreed with everything he had concluded. She had her technicians going over the car with a fine-toothed comb, she told him. There were no fingerprints at all on the steering wheel and front dash, so the chances were that someone had wiped it clean.

"If there is anything at all there, we'll find it. I've noted that we should compare what we found at the house with what we might find in the car," she said.

"You're a step ahead of me there," Jordan said. "I was going to go down to have a look, but I guess you'd rather I didn't."

"Keep away if you can. Let my lot do their jobs."

There was a meeting with the team so he could bring them up to date about everything, including his conversation with Frank Dirkin. "I don't know quite what to make of that. Mr Dirkin gave me the distinct impression that he thought the person in the car was a prostitute. We know Tracy took heavy-duty sleeping tablets but, really, would you have a working girl in the house when your wife is in her bedroom? I guess anything's possible, and it's our starting point."

John had been through the joint bank account. He had only found one thing vaguely suspicious.

"Stanley took voluntary redundancy from his last job. There was a small gap and then his salary from Better Print started coming in. They had a few thousand in the bank and their outgoings were not large. About six weeks ago, he started drawing out money in cash. That was new. Until then, it had all been card, direct transfer or online payments, and a bit of cash. About fifty quid at a time, until the change."

"What sort of amounts are we talking about?" Jordan asked.

"The maximum daily amount for a couple of days each week, five hundred. It adds up to quite a lot. I've put a spreadsheet in a team email."

"Okay. So, that screws up any chance of us finding out what he was spending the money on. What about the new care company?"

"Nothing that I could specifically say was them. But there are PayPal payments. I'm on to them to see if we can acquire more details."

"Putting two and two together, it has to be prostitutes, boss, doesn't it?" Vi said.

There was a murmur of agreement from others in the team.

"We must find that car, the one that arrived in the night, and we need to know where his own car was. It's looking as though he was transported in the boot. Did they take him from somewhere near his home or did he go and meet them? Sorry guys, but it's more screen watching. It's a pain, but it's paid dividends so many times before. You can do it."

"So, that's us definitely working over Christmas," John said.

"Find me the cars and you never know," Jordan answered.

"In two days. Huh, you'll be lucky."

"We'll give it our best shot," Kath said. "As you say, you never know."

"Look, I'll make sure everyone has some time off over the holiday. Put in whether you would prefer Christmas Eve, Christmas Day or Boxing Day, okay? That's the best I can do."

John swung his chair around to hunch over his keyboard. Jordan would need to have a word. He wasn't doing himself or his career any favours and needed to consider if it was worth it for the sake of a short holiday, even if it was with a new girlfriend.

Chapter 25

It was Kath who found it, which surprised no one. Over and over she had come up trumps with searches on CCTV footage. Vi said she had some sort of sixth sense. "She's a witch, that's what."

Kath laughed and said she had just referred to the email from the phone company identifying the last known location from his text messaging. She trawled the streets and roads around the location until the Astra had shown up on a weather camera on the M58.

"It's still bloody impressive, though," Vi said. "I mean, a white Vauxhall Astra. What are the chances?"

"I reckon I have to be good at something. I've done it so much since I went on light duties. It's like I've just developed a knack. A lot is to do with the timings. Plus, this was late, and the road was quiet. But apart from all that, I got off my lazy arse and went down to look at the car in the pound. I don't want to spoil your amazement at my magical skills, but it's got a bloody great sticker in the back window. A red *You'll Never Walk Alone* banner." She grinned. "I have to admit, it helped."

She printed out some images, the final one being the car at the huge supermarket car park just off Switch Island.

The team crowded around Kath's desk as she played the footage from the car park camera. The driver left the car and entered the mall. They watched as he ignored the opticians and key cutting. He didn't stop at the café or photo printers, and he did no shopping. He went into the toilets.

"That's it. We don't see him come out. I've watched right through to the next morning. His car sits there for ages. Obviously, you're not supposed to park there for hours, but nobody seems to have checked, and it's the middle of the night before there's any more activity with it. Winter time... who would be a security man patrolling a car park? You can't blame them for swerving the checks now and then."

They couldn't know whether Stanley had deliberately chosen a parking spot that was difficult to see from the CCTV, but he'd tucked the vehicle tightly into a corner. The view was restricted by a low hedge and a trolley bay. It wasn't possible in the dim lighting to tell who had driven it away, but there was no doubt two people were now in the front.

"Get that down to the technical lab and see if they can do anything about getting a clearer image. It's a long shot, but we know what colour his clothes were, so it could at least show us if it definitely wasn't Stanley," Jordan said.

"Already done, boss," Kath said.

There was a small buzz of excitement. It was a step forward, with the real possibility they had just seen the people who had taken their victim away.

Kath spoke up. "This was poor Mr Lipscowe on his way to Spencer's Lane bridge. I have still got to track that, and I'll put up some stills. Poor bugger must have been terrified if he had any idea what was in store for him."

They were glued to the images on the screen as Kath worked her magic. They saw it turn out of the car park and back towards Aintree. "That's not the right way," one of the civilian clerks said.

"Just wait," Kath said.

They saw him next on the traffic camera at Old Roan, opposite the station and the derelict pub. "The ANPR logged him there, but I'd got him already." He turned down Altway, and that was where they lost him. There was a groan from somewhere, and Kath laughed. "It doesn't matter. That takes him right to Bull Bridge Lane. They will have crossed the motorway there to get on the quieter side, and it's all over bar the shouting."

"We need to get back to the houses in Spencer's Lane where we found the car. It was the early hours, but we could be lucky. Fingers crossed for a baby," Jordan said, referring to a previous case, which was solved partly because of a sleepless mother gazing out of her window.

"John, contact the press department. See if they can arrange anything for the *Echo* and *Look North*. 'Did you see anything unusual' – that sort of thing and, if possible, roadside notices aimed at both carriageways. It's a long shot, but you never know."

The day had flown past. They had made valuable progress. "Put a rush on the image enhancement, will you? Stress that we can't wait until after the weekend. This could be a murderer we're looking at. In at the usual time tomorrow, guys, but we're moving on, it's been good work today."

"Yeah, thanks to our CCTV witch. I'll stand you a drink on the way home, mate," Vi said as she gave Kath a hug.

"You're on," she said. "Will you join us, boss?"

"Sorry, not tonight. I've got some stuff to do. But tomorrow for sure. Stel, do you want to come in my car and then you can get a taxi later?"

As he spoke, Jordan could have bitten off his tongue. He saw the sneaky glances, and the raised eyebrows. Most people knew Penny had gone to London with their little boy, and he sighed as Stella blushed and hustled from the room. They could never completely quash the idea that there was something more than being work colleagues between them. This time, he acknowledged it was his own fault. Because he was innocent, he couldn't imagine anyone seeing guilt.

Chapter 26

Stella was waiting by the car when he joined her. "Stupid sods. Did you see their faces? Pillocks. It does my head in, it really does," she said.

"It was my fault, sorry. You know you're just going to have to get yourself a boyfriend. It's the only answer."

Jordan kept his face straight as he spoke, but she knew him well and saw the twinkle in his eye.

"Bog off. Anyway, chance'd be a fine thing. When am I supposed to have any sort of relationship? What with the job, the house refurb – which is finished, thank God – and my family, I haven't got time to even do online dating. Not that I'd want to get into that."

She gave a little shuffle of her shoulders and slid into the car.

He climbed in beside her and decided that silence was the best defence, and they pulled out into a damp and dreary Copy Lane.

"So, where are we going and what have you got in those bags?"

"It's just some bits and pieces I want to drop off on the way home. Nothing terribly exciting, I'm afraid. Won't take long."

He drove the familiar route toward the Lipscowes' address. She turned to frown at him as he pulled up at the house opposite.

"You can stay here if you like. I'll just be a minute."

"No, you're alright, I'll come."

He jiggled the letter box cover on Frank Dirkin's door. The green curtains twitched and after a minute, the light in the hall was switched on. There was a rattle as Frank slid the chain across and peered at them through a small gap.

"Sort of time is this to be bothering folk? You didn't leave nothing if that's what you're thinking. What do you want now? Couldn't you ring? Come back tomorrow?"

Jordan held up the bags. "Don't want to disturb you, Mr Dirkin. Only my wife went away this morning and I've got this stuff, and I wondered if you could use it. With the weather being dodgy. I thought it might save you going to the shops."

"Eh. What are you talking about?"

"Just some stuff. There's a beef stew I made. It needs to be eaten today or tomorrow. There's some cereal, my little lad usually has it and it'll go stale by the time they get back. Some eggs. Oh, just stuff that'll go to waste."

The door opened, and the old man peered into the darkness.

"Shall I carry them through for you? Stick 'em in your kitchen?"

Frank moved aside, still frowning.

Jordan stepped through the door and down the hallway. He placed the bags on the work surface. "Couple of bottles of beer in there, Frank. I know you said you hadn't got anything in and it's been such rotten weather. You with your arthritis. I don't suppose you want to be out in it."

"I can't pay you?"

Jordan shook his head. "No, really, you'll be doing me a favour. I can't have it cluttering up the kitchen. I need to clear it out."

"Oh well, in that case, I suppose I could take it off your hands."

"This is my colleague, by the way, DS May. Let her give you her card and if you think of anything that might help us with the carry-on across the road, you could call either of us. We'll let you get on, don't want to bother you anymore."

Back in the car, Stella didn't speak for a minute and then she turned to look at Jordan. "What was all that?"

"I noticed the other day that his fridge was empty, and I just thought it'd save him going to the shops."

"Boss, that was a bloody lovely thing to do. You know it's not because he hasn't been out. He could have deliveries. He more than likely hasn't got the money. If he had kids, or was receiving credit, they might have put him in touch with a food bank. People like him, though, are too proud to ask. Yeah, that was a lovely thing to do."

"No, just paying it forward, as they say. I'm lucky I've got a family. He's a lonely old bloke. He used to have a wife and a life and now he hasn't even got a drink in for Christmas. It's not a big deal. Tell you what, though, I'd prefer if you didn't mention it to anyone. Okay?"

"But you're going to be on your own, with Penny gone."

"Yeah, but it's not the same. I'll be working. Not the same thing at all."

* * *

The house was warm from the central heating and lights had turned on automatically. But Jordan felt the emptiness as he walked through the door, even though Stella was with him.

There was no smell of cooking, no giggling from the bathroom, and no radio playing quietly in the kitchen. He threw off the feeling and turned to take Stella's coat. "Make yourself at home. I won't be long. Do you want wine or beer?"

"Did you say curry?"

"Yeah, beef, if that's okay?"

"Brilliant. In that case, I'll have a beer."

He wasn't gone long and by the time Jordan came back from the kitchen, Stella had turned on some lamps and the faux coal fire was flickering in the grate.

"Curry's in the microwave, rice is in the cooker and in a couple of minutes we can have some of Nana Gloria's garlic flatbread to keep us going," said Jordan.

"You're so organised. I make do with the chippy, toast, or cereal. I'm a disgrace. Sometimes I eat in the canteen instead of bothering at home. I'm so useless. If it wasn't for my mam's Sunday dinners, I'd never have any decent scran."

"Cooking for yourself isn't very satisfying, and we always have loads of stuff in the freezer. Anyway, while we're waiting, do you want to tell me what you've got on this bloke and your uncle?"

"I've printed out some stuff. Can I set it out here?"

"Yes, go on, get it out. The stuff's nearly ready to dish up and we'll eat first, if you like. Do you want another beer? You're not driving, so don't worry."

It was cosier now and, with the hot meal inside him and a couple of glasses of lager, Jordan relaxed. There was a message on his phone from Penny, to let him know they were safe, and a picture of Harry sitting with his cousins watching cartoons.

Chapter 27

They finished the meal, had some ice cream and shortbread biscuits, and Jordan poured them both a hefty measure of single malt. He picked up a couple of printouts from the table. Stella pointed out where documents showed that Carl had insured the car showroom heavily. It was not long before he locked it up and stuck a sign in the window saying 'closed for repairs'. He had continued to pay the instalments for the insurance cover. According to the fire department, vandals had started the fire. They found evidence of fireworks and an accelerant. There was no CCTV and no witnesses.

"What a surprise that must have been." Stella gave a snort of disgust. "They had no real choice but to come to that conclusion."

Jordan studied the reports and shook his head. "I can't believe they paid. This is so obviously a scam," he said.

Stella shrugged. "No choice, had they? He was insured for vandalism, and it was vandalism. He had a mate giving it a quick shufty every few days, so they couldn't say it was abandoned. Where the vandals came from and who put them up to it is anybody's guess, but it doesn't take a mastermind to put two and two together and come up with four."

There was another small sheaf of paper. He picked that up and frowned as he read about another fire. The blaze was in a house in Knotty Ash. This was after Carl had started a building and refurbishment company, Reybuild. They had already gutted the place, supposed to be getting it ready for refurbishment. They put it down to an electrical fault, and he claimed on his insurance. Because the place was only really a shell, he didn't get that much for the damage to the house. But he claimed for building supplies and equipment. There was a bit of discussion about just what had been in there, but he convinced them and they paid up. He'd bought the property from an old man who was going into care and paid peanuts for it.

Stella related a difficult phone conversation she'd had with the niece. The family was upset and felt that Carl was pestering the old man. They tried to warn him not to sign anything and contacted the local police. They said there was nothing they could do. The bloke owned the house, and it was up to him what he did with it. She was understandably bitter, wanting to know how come they were showing interest now when it was too late, and the old fella was dead. She had even spoken to the local social services, but by the time they even got around to speaking to him, it was too late. Her uncle had sold it and Reybuild had the deeds. He made a profit. "It's not going to be difficult to have an electrical fault in a place you're knocking about, is it? It wasn't strictly illegal, but it was definitely not on," she said.

"And the other one?" Jordan said.

This was another Reybuild property that had been raided by the Border Force. Neighbours reported seeing a lot of men going in and out. When they got in, they found a stinking dormitory – hugely overcrowded, filthy, and a health hazard. They took the blokes away and Stella was still trying to find out what happened to any of them. It could take months and she had reached the conclusion that they already knew the story.

Jordan nodded. "Asylum seekers or something like that. Poor sods being fleeced yet again. Unless it was more innocent than that, and it was a squat. Homeless people."

"That's not what the report says, though. The men had been paying rent."

"Was he operating on his own during all of this?"

"No, there were others involved – the directors of the building company, which is now dissolved, and partners in the car place. I've got a list here of names. Some of them are known to us and some I haven't been able to find anything on. I can't ask for access to his bank, of course, so most of this is from calling in favours and public record. Top and bottom of it is, though, he's a thug, a fly-by-night and a chancer. I haven't seen any mention of my Uncle Geoff, but I'll tell you, boss, I was nervous looking through it all."

She stopped and collected the papers and stuffed them into her bag. "Anyway, he vanished for a bit and now he's back. Somehow I reckon he's found out about my win. Obviously, he wouldn't approach me directly, but he probably sees Geoff as a soft touch. Which he is, and I'll bet he's the one who's been blabbing about lotteries and whatnot. It goes without saying that I'm not getting involved, but how can I stop Geoff? My granda's getting on, he's over ninety now, it would kill him to see his son in the dock."

"I think we have to find this bloke and have a sharp word, eh?" Jordan said.

He poured a second glass of whisky and they tried to move away from the worry with chat about other things. When Jordan's phone rang, they grimaced. "Neither of us can drive," he said.

The call was from a constable on the late shift, tasked with answering calls, along with a few others who were happy to do overtime after the appeal on the television for witnesses at the Spencer's Lane bridge.

Jordan grinned at her when he finished the call. "We've got a couple of witnesses. They've agreed to come in tomorrow morning for a chat."

"Excellent. Jesus, have you seen the time? It's after midnight. I'd better get off home. We'll need to be there when they arrive."

"Stay. The guest room's made up; it always is. You can get some kip now and we'll go in together in the morning."

She raised her eyebrows at him. "Do you think that's wise, us arriving together?"

"Oh, sod 'em, Stella. You can't live your life worrying about stories that other people invent."

Chapter 28

Jordan woke to the sound of rain on the windows and the swish of car tyres on the road outside. Even before he opened his eyes, he had remembered that the other side of the bed would be cold, and Harry wasn't going to come bouncing in with teddies and giggles. But he heard the shower in the guest room en suite and it helped.

He made them French toast and coffee.

"It's Christmas Eve tomorrow," Stella said. "I'll be over at my mam's. We do the mince pies together and make the stuffing for the bird, prepare some veggies, and loads of stuff like that. Done it for years, ever since I was a little kid. We have sherry and listen to carols. None of us are religious, but you don't have to be to enjoy all that, do you?"

"No, of course not. Nana Gloria and my mum go to the church with one of my brothers, but everyone else just stays at home and has a drink and a laugh. Have you decided what you're going to do about Christmas Day?"

"Yeah. If Geoff is going to be there, I'm not. It'd be horrible. I'd be on edge all the time. I wouldn't put it past him to put me on the spot and ask me for help in front of everyone. That'd make me look a dick."

"Come here. I'm not doing a turkey or anything and I'm going to be in working in the morning; if anything breaks on the case that'll take precedence, but you'd have some company."

"I'd like that. Can I let you know tomorrow night? Or will that be too late?"

"No, as I say, there'll be no Christmas dinner, but you don't need to be on your own. Unless you'd rather be, of course."

"No, it'd be rotten. I was dreading it, to tell you the truth."

It was just after half past six when they arrived at Copy Lane, and they were first in the incident room. A couple of uniformed officers saw them but there was just a simple good morning. Stella breathed a sigh of relief.

By the time Olive and Lesley Fox arrived, the room was buzzing. A list was being prepared to allocate cover and time off. John had called in sick. "Covid, according to HR," Vi said. Nobody voiced their thoughts, but there were sideways glances and frowns. "Tomorrow you can all take the day, providing you're available. That means no heavy drinking, I'm afraid," Jordan said. "We're interviewing witnesses this morning and it's always possible it'll lead to something. I would like everyone in on Monday but if you roll in a bit late, nobody is going to say anything. It's the best I can do."

As he passed Kath's desk, he paused. "Do you have someone to be with? I know the hospital messed up your plans."

"Yes, I'll go to my daughter's as we'd arranged. Thanks for asking, boss."

"Listen, don't worry too much about having to come in. It would only be if we had to mobilise and, with respect, you are better working from the office."

"Useless old cripple, you mean?"

"No, I don't mean that. I just mean that you're not going to be running up and down wet streets in the rain chasing bad guys, so, you know, chill. Enjoy what you can."

"Thanks, boss. But if you need me, call me in."

"I will."

* * *

Olive and Lesley Fox were nervous, but Olive particularly was excited to be in the interview room. It was easy to see that they had never been in the back of a police station before. Olive's gaze flipped from side to side, stopping to peer at the recording equipment on the table. Someone had given them tea, and she sipped and dabbed at her lips with a small white handkerchief. She smiled at the uniformed constable at the door and smoothed her already-tidy hair. Her husband Lesley crossed his arms and scowled at the floor, glancing up as Jordan and Stella entered the room and took seats on the other side of the table.

They introduced themselves and asked for permission to record the interview. Olive slid to perch on the edge of her seat, eyes wide, her body tense.

"Thank you so much for coming in. It's a busy time for everyone," Stella said. "Maybe the best thing would be if you tell us in your own words just what you saw."

Olive took a deep breath. "Lesley said we shouldn't come, shouldn't bother you. Didn't you?"

Lesley sniffed and nodded once.

"But I said to him, Lesley, you just never know. We thought about it and then we came."

"And we're grateful," Stella said. "So, if you could tell us just where and what happened, and then we can let you get on your way."

"Oh, we don't mind. There's no rush. We're just here to help. Aren't we, Les?"

Lesley nodded.

"So, on the way back from visiting my cousin Lynne, he took a wrong turn. Not because he was drunk. Did I say that? Anyway, we ended up going round and round in circles. We were trying to find our way back to the motorway. Which one is it, Les?"

Les sighed and stared at his wife.

"The M57, was it?" Stella said.

"Oh, yes. We used to know our way around, but we moved away, and things have changed. It wasn't Lesley's fault." She reached across to lay a hand on top of her husband's. He shrugged it off.

"So, the bridge?" Jordan said.

"Yes, well, that doesn't get you there, does it?"

"No. But you saw something?"

"We did. I said to Les that I thought it was disgusting at that time of night. Men in that condition should be ashamed. We all like a drink, but they were so drunk one of them couldn't even walk. There were two of them holding him up as they went along the road. I don't know where they thought they were going so late."

"What time was it?" Jordan opened the file in front of him and picked up his pen. Maybe it would move things along if Olive Fox saw he was serious.

"It was late," she said. "We didn't mean to be that late. But our Lynne, she'd gone on and on and in the end…"

"Half past two, thereabout." Lesley's quiet interruption took them all by surprise.

"Excellent. Can either of you describe the men?"

Lesley shook his head and went back to studying the floor tiles.

"They were wearing dark clothes. They weren't dressed up. Just ordinary, maybe jeans and dark jackets. One of them, the really drunk one, didn't even have a jacket on. I bet he was sorry the next day. Stupid going out in that weather with no coat. Asking for trouble."

Eventually they had a vague description of three ordinary-looking men, ordinary clothes, average height. One of them was bald, but the only thing outstanding was the condition of the one in the middle.

"Did you see any cars around?" Jordan asked.

"A white Vauxhall parked on the grass." Lesley didn't speak often, but when he did, his comments made a difference.

"There was another one parked at the side, a dark one. A Fiesta."

Olive wasn't to be silenced. "'That's odd,' Lesley said to me, 'look at that, somebody hanging around this time of night. That's dodgy.' Didn't you, Les?"

Lesley nodded.

"That's really why we came. I said to him 'Do you remember that car, Les?' The lights were on inside and somebody at the wheel. 'That's odd,' I said. Something like that really does make you wonder what's going on, doesn't it?"

There wasn't much more, though Olive could have filled the morning with her opinions and her thoughts.

"You've been very helpful," Jordan said. "Thank you. Are you alright getting home?"

"We're not going home. We're on our way to our Lynne's for Christmas. Aren't we, Les?"

Lesley sighed, nodded and closed his eyes.

It wasn't much, but it was a lot more than they had before. At the door, Lesley Fox stopped and turned around.

"Was there something else?" Stella asked.

"Merry Christmas," Lesley said. Then they left.

Jordan and Stella sat for a minute in silence.

"That Lesley, eh?" Stella said.

"Proper live wire," said Jordan.

"Actually, though, what he told us..."

"Yep, the dark-coloured Fiesta. It's relevant. I reckon we've got time to get a coffee and a mince pie first, though."

Chapter 29

There had been no other valuable responses to the call for witnesses. Jordan scanned the notes. There were the usual comments about police inefficiency, and the constant complaints about danger to the public in the absence of bobbies on the beat. There were a couple of sightings of cars in the area – delivery vans and children on bikes – but none of them were the right time or the correct area. They only had Olive and Lesley, but it wasn't nothing.

John had been tasked with following up on care providers, and now, in his absence, Kath took over from where he'd left off. After an hour, she came to stand beside Jordan's desk. "He's done a good job, boss. Seems like he's spoken with all the companies in the area. He's even been able to get a list of cars driven by all the staff who worked in that area. There's a whole range, of course. They use their own cars, though. The companies have details for insurance. There are Fiestas in the mix. I'm not sure how much this is going to help us. Your old man, Frank, is it? He says that he saw a car and then a van, but Tony Yates says that all he saw was Stanley's car on that night. I suppose carers sometimes use a different vehicle for all sorts of reasons. Okay, the car is suspicious coming late at night and then, you know, the bedroom light and all that but, he's an old man. How reliable is he?"

Jordan brought her a chair, and they went through the reports again. She was right; it was like looking for a needle in a haystack when you didn't know what sort of needle it was and whether it was actually in the haystack at all. "Do you not think that the next-door neighbour could be more help?"

Jordan blew out his cheeks. "I'll call her again, but unless she's actually hiding something, it doesn't seem as though she really knew who the carer was over the last few weeks."

"Bit odd, though, given she was supposed to be so close to Tracy Lipscowe."

"I have the feeling that the friendship was under strain. She hadn't seen Stanley for a while and didn't know who was cleaning the house or even if anyone was. Maybe, now that Tracy was becoming more and more infirm, they didn't see as much of each other. It's sad, but I reckon it happens. I'm not suggesting anyone's to blame. We all have to live our own lives. I'll have another word, though. What about the van?"

Kath shook her head. "As you know, there are no cameras in the road, so I can't start from there, and the entire country is awash with white VW vans, especially those Transporters. They use them for everything, even campers. I've tried, but there's nothing on the night of the murder that I've been able to find. Nothing near the house and I looked at the area around the bridge, but again, nothing. That time of the night, I'd have expected it to be fairly simple. I followed the roads from Switch Island and then the routes from the city centre. It's a lot and I haven't quite finished but, unless they took a very odd route, it's not there. I've asked the SOCO team and Ted Bliss, but nobody in the area had a security camera."

"That was a good idea. Shame it didn't pay off."

"Maybe you could ask the neighbour next door if she remembers a van at another time. It's frustrating."

"Yes, I will. I'll ring Tony Yates in Spain as well. Thanks, Kath."

Tony Yates's phone didn't ring. There was no invitation to leave a message. It couldn't be helped, and now they would have to wait until he came back from his holiday.

Chapter 30

Penny understood. She didn't send videos of the women laughing and cooking in Jordan's mum's kitchen. She didn't take images of the family sitting around the table, passing the dishes back and forth. He knew how it would be. He had been there. She sent a picture of Harry in his pyjamas, drifting off to sleep, and a simple message.

Missing you. Coming home soon.

Before he left that morning, he had taken a lasagna out of the freezer to defrost. It wouldn't take long to heat through, then he could sit in the living room and put on some music. Otherwise, he could spread his papers out on the dining table and read as he ate. His options were limitless.

He pulled out onto Copy Lane, heading for home. A quick glance at his watch and he turned left instead of right, earning a blast from the horn of the car behind him. There was a brief detour to the Chinese restaurant, where he ordered ribs and sweet and sour chicken. He added fried wantons, egg fried rice, noodles, and they gave him fortune cookies in light of the season.

The smell in the car reminded him just how hungry he was. When he arrived at Frank Dirkin's house, he had a moment of misgiving. Maybe the old bloke had plans. Maybe he was visiting friends or a group he was a part of. He shrugged. It didn't matter, really. The food wouldn't go to waste.

He knocked on the door. The curtains twitched.

"You again, don't you have a bloody home to go to?" Frank growled.

"I do, but nobody there, Frank. Couldn't face it. I brought Chinese and this." He held up the bottle of single malt from the supermarket.

"For Christ's sake, what am I, your nanny? Come on in, you wet blanket."

Frank dragged plates out of the sideboard. He wiped them with a dishcloth. He pulled out two heavy tumblers and polished them with the same cloth. Then he laid the table. There was no comment, but he used what was obviously his wife's best china. He stood for a moment looking down at it and, for the first time since Jordan had met him, he smiled.

"She loved this set."

They didn't have much in common. Frank tried to talk to Jordan about the football, and it quickly fizzled out. He didn't have much to say about cricket. Frank had worked in an engineering factory. That world was a mystery to Jordan. The decision to come here had been partly altruistic and partly selfish. Jordan had assumed the man would be alone. There were other places he could have gone and been welcomed. But they were places where family would be gathered, and that wasn't what he needed right now. He hadn't come here to work. He didn't intend to, but with nothing else to discuss, they began to talk about the neighbours.

Frank and his wife had lived in the house for three decades. He'd seen dozens of people come and go. They had enjoyed an active social life, drinks, and parties, even holidays with people they were close to.

"My mate Bill, he were great fun. We went to the match together. People could afford it in those days, now you have to be a bloody millionaire. But we went and the girls would go shopping. Then we'd go out for a bevvy and some chips afterwards. We went on holiday together a couple of times. Scotland. Devon once. Good memories."

As Frank took a drink and held out his glass for a fill, Jordan saw the glint of sadness in his eyes.

"Are they still around?"

The old man shook his head. "Not here anymore. They moved a while back. Needed a bungalow because Veronica couldn't manage the stairs. I see 'em once now and then but it's not the same, is it?"

"No, I don't suppose it is."

"Now I think about it, he had one of them carers. Veronica had an operation. She didn't qualify for the council ones, but Bill couldn't be doing with housework, giving her a bath, changing beds and whatnot. He advertised in the paper. It wasn't any good, though. He didn't keep 'em long." Frank gave a snort of a laugh. "They didn't enjoy having strangers in the house all the time. Said they couldn't settle to it."

The whisky had relaxed them both, and Jordan asked if he could leave the car there until the morning and call a taxi. "I didn't mean to stay this long, or drink this much, mate. I'm over the limit."

Frank leaned forward and patted Jordan on the knee. "You've brightened my night, lad. It's been lovely. I know there's nothing to be done about being on my own and I've not done so badly since I lost my Gladys, but Christmas time, no matter how hard you try, you feel it. I'll be fine now. There's this evening to look back on, and some of that stuff left over to eat tomorrow. I'll be ace. You're a busy man and you've got a family of your own and all that, but if you can, call in now and then, just to say 'how do'."

Chapter 31

Frank's house was still in darkness when Jordan arrived in a taxi to collect his car. He pushed a last-minute Christmas card through the letter box.

Even though Christmas Eve was an ordinary day for many of the officers, especially the ones in uniform, there was still a different atmosphere in the station. The women in the canteen were wearing reindeer antlers, and a couple of the civilian clerks had dressed as elves.

There were already drunks in the cells and the custody sergeant was morose and short-tempered, looking forward to a difficult day and worse evening.

They still had no success searching for the elusive white VW Transporter and Jordan tried Tony Yates's mobile number again on the off chance that the signal had been the problem and might have recovered from the day before. But there was still nothing.

"I don't know exactly when he's due back. I'm not sure he'll be able to tell us anything more than he already did, but it would be good to confirm what we have. We should have been able to find the vehicle. The roads were quiet because it was the middle of the night. I had another word with old Frank yesterday and he is still insistent that he saw a small dark-coloured car and, later on, the white van. One of them must have got the timing or the day wrong."

"If we find out which airline he travelled with, maybe we'll track him down," Kath said.

"Yeah, but we don't even know if he went with a tour group or whatever," Jordan said.

"Leave it with me, boss. I've got a couple of ideas."

The calls following the appeals in the paper and the television had dried up, and there was very little happening. By mid-afternoon Jordan decided they might as well call it a day.

"I need a while," Kath said. "If you're going to the pub, I'll see you there. I don't want to give up on this just now."

Some of the staff had left their cars at home and were planning a bit of a session, but when he got to the pub, Jordan ordered half a pint of lager and drank it slowly. He put money behind the bar so if they wanted to they could have a bit of a blowout. He received a cheer for that. They followed it with a jeer when he reminded them that they were in the middle of a case.

Stella slid into the seat beside him. "I rang John, boss."

"Okay... and?"

"You ought to know. He's definitely got Covid. Sounded bloody awful on the phone and he sent me a picture of his test. He's proper gutted." She grinned. "I know I shouldn't say it, but he was such a whinge. I reckon it's comeuppance."

"Well, maybe. But it's good to know he wasn't skiving. He's a good copper most of the time. I'm not staying long, Stel. Possibly not much point, but I thought I'd have another drive round by the Lipscowes'. Most people will be home for the holidays by now and there's the off chance the white van is local. It's probably too tall for the garages around there. Maybe it's parked on a drive. I'll see you tomorrow, unless there's anything in the meantime. Just before I leave, I'm going to give Vickie Frost a call, though. I was banking on a more in-depth report from forensics, but I guess it's a forlorn hope now until Monday at the earliest."

Kath limped quickly across the pub towards them. She sat on a chair dragged from another table and leaned in towards Jordan. "What are you drinking, Kath?" Stella asked. "The boss has put money in for us."

She ordered a prosecco and pulled her tablet from the oversized bag hanging on the back of her chair. "I was in touch with a mate at the airport. He spoke to a border force colleague, and they found our man on the computer. Thing is, though, boss, I thought you said he was going to Spain with a group of mates?"

"Yes, that's it."

"He's a big bloke?"

"A big bloke and he most likely had a bag with him and a puffa coat."

She opened an image on her tablet. "Is that him?"

"Yeah."

"He was checking in for a flight to France. So, either there was a very last-minute change of plans, or he was lying to you." She raised her glass in a toast and gulped back a mouthful of sparkling wine.

"France." Jordan frowned and stared into the dregs of his drink. "Definitely told me Spain, and with mates. Why the hell would he want to lie about that? Although, I suppose, he could have still got there but with a change of flights."

"There's more, though," Kath said. "Do you see the woman behind him?"

Jordan leaned closer to the screen and nodded.

"I've viewed all the footage I can of him in the airport, and she is there on almost everything. They are not obviously together. They don't talk or share snacks or anything like that, but wherever he is, she is. At one point, he goes to the gents, and she stands by the wall until he comes out. He doesn't speak to her, but I'm sure she follows him back to the seating area. They sit a bit apart, they walk separately, but there is something about their behaviour that puts them together."

"Can your mate find out who she is?"

"He can and he has. Kylie Heywood. Liverpool girl. I haven't had the chance to do much more research yet.

Didn't want to miss the party." She raised her glass and grinned.

"That's really excellent work, Kath. So, what is he up to going to France with a woman, not Spain with a gang of mates?"

Vickie from forensics chose that moment to ring. There was laughter and music in the background, but Vickie was her quiet self when she spoke. "I thought you'd be off home soon and wanted to check in," she said. "I have a bit of information to pass on before I get into the Christmas spirit."

"Okay, go on," Jordan said.

"It's about the car. We found mud on the carpet in the driver's footwell. We've sent some off to the university. It might give us a clue where the bloke was before he met up with the victim. It's different from the stuff in the boot, where we now reckon they had stuffed your poor bloke. So, there's that. Also, we found a couple of hairs. This was interesting. They matched hair found at the house. Long black. I would say it was female, but we'll wait for confirmation of that. One was in the boot, too."

"What's your take on that?"

"Could be a couple of things. Either the shedder had done something in the boot, like taken out shopping, that sort of thing – feasible, if she was a carer – or the hair was originally on the clothes or body of Stanley Lipscowe, and it came off while he was in there. So, there's something for you to ponder over the weekend. Your wife's away, so it'll keep you out of mischief."

He ended the call. "Kath, that woman. She's got dark hair, hasn't she?"

"Yep."

"Would you call it long?"

"I'd say shoulder length. Some people might call that long, especially if theirs is very short."

Jordan thought about Vickie and her boyish, blond style. She was right. It was something to ponder and, as he left the pub, Jordan's mind was swirling with the new developments. He had needed something new and there it was.

Chapter 32

Jordan had FaceTime with Penny and Harry. The little boy couldn't sit still. In the end, they cut it short. "We're coming back the day after tomorrow," Penny said.

"I thought you were staying until Wednesday."

"Yes, but without you, it's not the same. I came as much for Nana Gloria and your mum, so they could be with Harry. They understand. Anyway, our Lizzie has asked me to go over there, with you as well, of course. She said she'd put on a roast dinner, and we can pretend it's Christmas. I don't think that will work, but it'll be nice. Will you be able to do that?"

"Yes, that'll be lovely. I don't really know how much good it's done staying here, but I know I wouldn't have been able to settle being so far away."

"Not much progress, then?"

"Some, but just as many puzzles. Have a lovely day tomorrow and I can't wait for you to be back."

There were a couple of presents under the tiny tree they had in the corner, but he decided he'd wait now until his family were home before he opened them. He put another one at the front with Stella's name on the label.

His mind was going over and over the new information as he ate the lasagna he had planned for yesterday, drank some wine and made notes.

The hair. There were quite a few explanations for that. He would ask Florence McGrady if she was aware of a carer with long black hair. He would call Vickie on

Tuesday and ask her to double check the forensic evidence from the guest room. She may not have had time to read the comments from Frank about the night-time visitor. If the hair was in the bedroom, then the idea that it had been on Stanley's clothes made all of that so much clearer. In Jordan's mind, there was little doubt that the night-time visitor had been providing carer services of quite another kind.

Chapter 33

Jordan slept well. He had turned off his computer and put the notes away an hour before he went to bed. He read a book he'd had on the bedside table for ages. Lee Child was his go-to author and although he liked his life most of the time, he could see the attraction of setting off and wandering with no real direction. America was the place to do that, though, maybe Australia. He didn't think there were enough places in England to get lost in. As always, by the end of the book, the bad guys were dealt with and Reacher was back on the road. He turned off the light and was asleep within minutes.

The morning could have felt lonely and depressing, but he was prepared for it. Knowing tomorrow would be the last day he would wake up alone cheered him anyway, but he was out of bed as soon as he opened his eyes, had a long hot shower and then went down to the kitchen to turn on the coffeemaker and fry up bacon, eggs, mushrooms, and tomatoes.

The dishes were in the dishwasher, jazz was playing on the music system, and he was kneading pastry, cooking chicken and chorizo, mushrooms, and herbs. Pasties might not be traditional Christmas Day food, but it wouldn't matter what time Stella arrived. He could just put them straight into the oven while they had a drink.

Once the cooking preparation was done and a salad made, he spread his paperwork out on the table again. It was mid-morning, and he probably had a couple of hours to study all the information and plan the next moves.

Stella arrived earlier than expected. Her eyes were red and shadowed. She threw her jacket onto the hook in the hall, dropped her bag on the floor, and kicked off her shoes. She held out a bottle of red wine and one of Pusser's Rum.

Jordan didn't speak. He poured her a glass of wine, which she drank in two huge gulps. Once she had perched on the edge of the settee, he sat opposite to her and raised his eyebrows. "Okay, you going to tell me?"

"Bloody Uncle Geoff."

Jordan had already guessed that part. The rest of the story was delivered in short bursts interspersed with many and varied expletives and heavy gulps of another glass of wine. Geoff had turned up unexpectedly, but of course it wasn't so unexpected. Everyone knew the Christmas Eve routine at Stella's mums. Geoff had tried repeatedly to corner Stella on her own and when that didn't work, had muscled in while she sat with her granddad just before she left.

"He knew it would be hard for me to tell him to get stuffed with Granda sitting there. He was all smarm and smiles. Full of the plans for this bloody building development and the opportunity and how he only needs a few thou." Suddenly, the tension overflowed and tears rolled down her cheeks. "Sorry, Jordan. I haven't slept and I'm a mess. It ended with a huge row, and I left my mam in tears and my granda shaken and upset. Bloody great, isn't it? Christmas Day and the family are furious with me. But that's not the end of it."

She held out her phone. "This was on my phone when I got out of bed this morning." The message wasn't very long.

Stel. Sorry about yesterday. I'm stuck, queen. I have to give him what he's asking for. There's no choice. Please. You can afford it. Do it for my dad. Please. Geoff.

Chapter 34

Jordan handed the phone back and Stella clicked the off button and flung it onto the sofa cushion beside her.

"Let's eat," Jordan said.

She frowned at him, expecting and hoping for a comment, but the pasties smelled delicious and she'd had no breakfast.

He waited until she had begun the smoked salmon salad before he said anything. "I think that's a bit sinister. Have you thought about what you're going to do next?"

She swallowed and frowned at him. "Sinister?"

"Yes, it doesn't sound as if he's asking for a favour. It seems to me that it's more that he's afraid. Maybe desperate."

"I hadn't thought of it that way. I just felt like he was putting pressure on. Now you mention it, though, I see what you mean."

"If I'd seen that in connection with a case, blackmail would be the first thing that leapt out at me. I reckon it would have been the same for you, if you weren't so close. That's the issue with this. You're too close. You're involved."

"That's all very well. What am I supposed to do?"

"Do you want me to have a word with him? I can talk to Geoff. Or I could have a little chat with this other bloke. Carl, is it? Do you know where he lives, or where I can find him?"

He placed a board on the table filled with the pasties and sauté potatoes. She took one and for a while there was silence. "God, they're gorgeous. Can I have another?" She took another and placed it on the plate in front of her. She wiped her mouth with the napkin. It was all playing for time and Jordan knew that. She knew he knew. She sighed and then nodded.

"I feel pathetic. I should just have said no straight off. Actually, to be fair, I did. If it hadn't been for Granda, I could handle this. I'd just tell him to bog off and leave me alone. This puts a different light on things, though."

She didn't need Jordan to tell her that giving in now was out of the question. They finished the food. He promised her coffee and chocolates later and, providing there was nothing that needed them to go out, a glass of whisky or maybe the special rum that she'd brought.

"We'll set up a meeting. My feeling is the other bloke is the one to target. That way, nothing is getting back to your family. Find out where and when we can find him and then let me know. Are you up for a walk now, though?"

She nodded. It was traditional, after all. A stroll on Christmas Day to help the food go down. It was a decent leg stretch to the beach and, although it was cold, it was pleasant to be out in the fresh air. "Were you planning on working this affie?"

Jordan nodded. "If you don't mind. We could go through what we have."

"I think that'd be great. It'll take my mind off the other stuff. But I just want to say thanks. Obviously for this and the scran, but as well if you have a word with Carl, it might be enough to fix it. Thing is, though, what if we find out he's blackmailing Geoff? What the hell could he have done to leave him open to that?"

"One step at a time, eh?"

It was warm back in the house and Jordan poured the rum and brought out a box of Swiss chocolates with a flourish. "Just because we're working doesn't mean we can't indulge."

They spread out the murder books and opened the laptops and, as the day slipped away, they read about dead bodies and the evil deeds they were witness to.

Chapter 35

Stella stayed over. There had been too much alcohol and by the time they had talked the case round and round, it was no longer Christmas Day.

The next morning was cold and wet again and had the dead feel of 'the day after'. They were quiet and hungover sitting at the table eating bacon baps. Once breakfast was eaten, Stella collected her belongings and got into her car. She waved once as she pulled away, heading for home to change and then onward to Copy Lane. "Best if we arrive separately, mate. No point feeding the rumour mill," Stella said.

Jordan filled his go-cup with strong black coffee and headed to Aintree. There had been three white vans parked up near the houses when he visited on Christmas Eve. One was a Ford Transit, and he dismissed it. The second was a VW Transporter, but it was a T4 – similar but not the same as the one they were looking for. There was one more. The correct model, but with images of balloons and flowers along the side – an advert for a flower shop. It was tucked down the side of an ordinary-looking house.

Feeling frustrated and impatient, he walked the short distance to Frank's house.

Frank nodded a greeting and moved aside to let him in. "Did you have a good day yesterday?" he asked.

"My friend came round. I missed the family, though. It was okay. I'm glad it's over and we can get back to normal."

"You and me both. What have you got there?" Frank waved at the white plastic carrier bag.

"Leftovers. You don't have to take them if you don't want. They'll freeze well for some time when you don't want to bother to cook."

He handed over the pasties and a slice of Christmas cake. "Thanks. It's hard. It's not that I can't afford food. I could, I could get myself some stuff. Simple stuff to fill my belly. Just can't be arsed. I never could cook much and I can't be doing with trailing round and round the shops. When every step's a knife through your knee, not much is fun anymore. I can't afford all them ready meals and you get sick of tins of soup and beans. My Gladys were a grand cook, so I never bothered."

"Have you never thought about meals on wheels?"

"Bloody Norah. I'm not going down that road. Before you know it, I'd have social services poking their noses in here, there and everywhere, wanting me in a home, and all of this sold off. No way. I know you mean well, lad. Don't think I don't appreciate it, I do, but I don't want the authorities involved. I'm not going to starve. Ha, especially not with these bad boys to tuck into."

"I still haven't solved that mystery of the van, Frank."

"What mystery?"

"The van you saw in the Lipscowes' drive the night they died. You said you'd seen a dark-coloured small car and then a van. You don't think it could have been a different day, do you?"

"Aye, I saw it on different days. I saw that car. I told you that anyway. Last Monday it were there. Didn't stay long and there were no lights on upstairs, not like before. Although…"

"Although?"

"You'll put this down to me being an old fart, I know, but there was a light. In the front room. What would be their main bedroom. But it was dim, not the big light. If I had to describe it, I would have said it was like a torch. But that's silly. Why I never mentioned it? Didn't make sense. There was no power cut or nothing like that. Then the light came on in the hallway, the door opened, light went out, car drove off. I'm sure as I'm standing here, that's what happened. Then a bit later – after I'd been for a pee – here comes a van. So, I don't know what your other witness said. Maybe they was telling porkies. Nowt as funny as folk. Have you thought of that?"

"I had, as a matter of fact."

"Don't know where it come from, mind. Only van I seen local like it, is round the corner. Parked up there a lot, it is. House looks empty, so I suppose somebody's just taking advantage."

Jordan drove away, his mind rolling this new information round and round. Everything Tony Yates had said was in doubt. His destination, his lonely travel. It was difficult at this stage to find a reason, but there was one, and it felt important.

It looked more and more as though Frank had been a witness to a murder, although he didn't know that. Jordan didn't see any point telling him right now. He may seem like a tough old boot, but you could never tell.

Chapter 36

The station was quiet, although there were several people in the detention suite due to overindulgence in the Christmas spirit.

Vi was in and checking through reports from the day before. Stella waved as Jordan dropped his briefcase and laptop in the tiny office. "Bit late, boss." She grinned as she called over to him.

"Alright, but I've been working. I did at least find a van. Might not be the right one, but I reckon it's worth investigating. Why don't the three of us get some coffee? I've brought Christmas cake and I'll bring you up to date. Is there anything from John?"

Both women shook their heads.

"No point me contacting DVLA until Wednesday. There's an extra day because of the twenty-fifth being a Sunday," Vi said.

"Yeah. I thought so. Trouble is, we really need to have a look at that van. It's odd that it's parked there as the house seems empty, but it would be difficult to call it abandoned. Do you think you could at least find out who owns the house? If it belongs to them, problem solved, we can try to find them or possibly get a warrant, given Frank is still insistent he saw a white van on the night of the murder."

"I can probably do that online, yes." Jordan updated the board with a printed image of the van. He sat at one of the empty desks and opened his laptop. His own office, cold and dull, didn't tempt him and he didn't need the privacy. He scrolled through reports that had come in over the past couple of days. Stella was pounding away on her keyboard, updating her own records. For a couple of hours, the room was relatively quiet with just the muffled sound of activity in the corridor and the swish of car tyres on the road outside.

Vi pushed back from her desk, "This cake's lovely, did you make it? Tell me you didn't. I can't do with a bloke being a better baker than me. Not unless he's a proper chef, at least," Vi said.

"You're off the hook. I helped, but really it was all down to Penny."

"Thank God."

Vi wanted to discuss how they had spent Christmas Day, and although Jordan and Stella had nothing to hide and nothing to be ashamed of, they didn't want to be in the position of having to say so. On the other hand, they didn't want to lie. They were relieved when Vi's phone rang and before she had finished talking to her husband about plans for dinner, they had cleared away the cups and were back behind their computers.

Stella sent Jordan a private message to let him know Carl had turned up at her mother's house the day before and invited himself to eat and drink with the family. Her mother had rung to apologise for her part in the family bust-up and complained about Geoff's friend, who had monopolised conversation and hung around until the early hours when he and Geoff had taken a taxi back to Geoff's flat.

> *I rang him there this morning and told him I wanted to see Carl. Could be I have given him the impression that I was coming round to the idea of putting up the money! Tomorrow at the Black Bull, half six. It's not far from that print shop, funnily enough. I think Carl lives near there. S.*

> *Okay. We'll go straight from work and sort him out. Try not to have your uncle along if you can swing it. I think it will go better if it's just Carl. J.*

Jordan took a call from Penny, letting him know she was back in Crosby. Leaving Stella and Vi with permission to go home as soon as they were ready, he shrugged into his overcoat. "Boss, just before you leave," Vi shouted across the room. "That house. The empty one. It belongs to Mrs Pauline Yates. It has her as the owner, but she died a year ago. I haven't been able to confirm it yet, but it could well be that it's in probate. According to a quick search on 192, Pauline Yates and Tony Yates lived at the same address. I intend to confirm that with the council, and I'm going to request a copy of the death certificate, but we'll have to wait until the offices open up again. There's not much more I can do, so I'm off home for leftovers and beer with my fella and the kids."

"You might as well all get off as soon as you've finished whatever it is that you're working on. Things are slow and there's nothing we can do about it." There was a mumble of approval and a general move to leave.

Chapter 37

As Jordan pulled into his drive, the door flew open and Penny stepped out. Harry jigged up and down, shouting and waving until he was allowed to run and show his daddy his new Superman outfit. Jordan picked up his little boy to swing him into the air. Everyone was laughing.

It was only when they were inside sharing a glass of fizzy wine and Jordan finally opening his presents from under the tree that he realised the one he had wrapped for Stella was still there. Penny picked it up and read the label. "Did you forget to take this into the office?"

Of course, she hadn't known whom he had spent Christmas Day with. For a moment he hesitated, but there was no reason to lie to his wife and it was something he had never done. She listened to his explanation quietly and looked down at the gift still in her hand.

"What are you going to do with this?"

"The moment has passed. She was so upset when she arrived, it just never happened," he said. "Here, give it to me." He tore off the wrapping and took out the fancy Jo Malone candle and positioned it on the mantlepiece.

"Do the others in the office know she was here? Why was she not with her family? Aren't they close?"

"There was only Vi today, and it didn't come up. She's been having some trouble with an uncle. It made things really unpleasant at her mother's, so I asked her round."

He knew he should let it drop now. It had been innocent. They had simply worked together. There was nothing to explain, nothing to deny. So why did he feel the urge to say so?

Penny turned the candle around with the fancy label facing the front. "You probably should be careful. There's already been talk." With that, she left the room and shortly afterwards he heard her stripping the bed in the spare room.

* * *

The next morning, while they had breakfast together, Penny gave him all the gossip from the family in London.

He made a detour on his way to work so he could check the van was still there, and that there was no sign of life in Tony Yates's house. The scene tape had gone from the Lipscowes' place. The house was dark and looked dejected, with the curtains part drawn in the downstairs rooms. He should make sure it was properly secured, maybe even have the windows boarded up. He sent a short text to Kath to follow it up. It would reflect badly on the force if the local yobs vandalized it. He knocked at the house next door and, in a replay of the situation just over a week ago, the bedroom window flew open and Flo McGrady, in shower cap and dressing gown, called down to him. "I'm just out the shower. Can you come back later?"

"I only have one quick question."

"Bloody hell, give me a minute."

She sighed and slammed the window closed. He wasn't invited in and had no choice but to speak to her on the doorstep. She pulled the collar of the dressing gown close around her neck and shivered theatrically.

He asked her about the white van. She shook her head slowly and pursed her lips. "Not in the garden, no. I've never seen one. Just the cars from the carers. There were deliveries now and then, like we all have, but they don't pull in, they just park. They park wherever they like, sometimes right on the corner. You lot should do something about that."

He asked about a white van at the house opposite, where Tony Yates lived. "Bloody hell, there's white vans everywhere, white ones, green ones, every colour under the sun. Especially just before Christmas, the place was awash with 'em. Yes, outside his house, outside my house, outside every bugger's house. But not in Tracy's garden. Now, if you don't mind, I've got things to do." She stepped back and pushed the door forward.

There was no choice but to walk away.

So, there was still only Frank insisting on the vehicle in the front space on the night of the murder. Still no answer to his calls to Tony Yates's phone. He had the distinct feeling that there was a connection, if he could winkle it out.

Chapter 38

Now that Christmas and Boxing Day proper were past, most of the team was back. A couple of civilian clerks had taken the extra day, but Vi was there, and Kath. Jordan hadn't been at his desk long before his phone rang with a call from John.

The detective constable apologised. "I know what it looked like, boss. I can tell you, though, I've been bloody awful. Shit Christmas, to be frank."

Jordan reassured him he believed he had the illness, that he'd seen the image of his test stick and he shouldn't worry.

"I'm still testing positive, but I'm feeling much better now. A bit wobbly if I try to do too much, but on the up. Bored out of my skull, though. I can't even go round the sales. Could you send me some work through and any reports I should see, to keep me up to date?"

"I'll make sure you see what there is. The white van is still a mystery, and the whereabouts of Tony Yates. Can't do much about that unless we can prove there's a genuine suspicion he's done something. At the moment, it's just a niggle. Let it mull and if you come up with any ideas, call me. I hope you're back in the office soon. Sorry about your Christmas plans."

"I've got a refund on my hotel money, anyway. They don't want you going if you've got the lurgy. So that worked out. We're planning on going later. Maybe for Easter, bad guys permitting."

"You're planning ahead then, with Millie?"

"She's great. We have fun. I like her a lot."

* * *

Jordan stood in front of the board. The picture of Stanley Lipscowe, broken and bloody, and that of his wife, grinning at them in happier times, had been surrounded by Post-it notes and jottings about vans and cars, drunken revellers on the bridge and cash withdrawals. On the other side was the name Tony Yates and a question mark.

Stella brought him a mug of coffee and came to stand beside him. "That money could have been to buy his wife some pressies," she said.

"I suppose. It seems like a lot. Have a word with Vickie Frost. I imagine they've already looked at the parcels from under the tree. Get an idea of how much they'd spent."

"That's bloody sad, isn't it?"

"It is. Listen, tonight, I reckon we should go to the pub in separate cars. It'll make it easier for going home afterwards, yeah?"

"Absolutely. I'm really grateful that you're doing this, boss."

"Not a problem. We'll just give him a bit of a scare and tell him to leave you and your uncle alone."

Half an hour before Jordan was due to leave for the face-off at the Black Bull with Carl Reynolds, John rang him.

"Tony Yates, boss. France on his own at Christmas seemed odd to me, so I had a word with a mate in border control."

Of course, Jordan thought, John hadn't seen the board with the notes about the woman. It was still unclear whether there was a connection, but they should add it to the online report, anyway. He'd do that first chance he had. "Are they working, then?"

"The tunnel bods are, so it didn't take him long. Now we've left the EU, you need to have your passport stamped as if you were going to bloody Africa or somewhere. Anyway. He came back to the UK. Christmas Eve, on the train."

"So, he's here somewhere. He's not at his house in Aintree, not unless he's in there with the lights off. There's something very wrong about him. I liked him when I first met him, but he's turning out to be dodgy. Just goes to show you. Thanks for this, John," Jordan said. "Take it easy and I'll look forward to seeing you back in work when you're well. One final thing before you go: can you check with your mate and see if he can confirm that Yates was on his own when he arrived? I realise it's tricky, but it might be important."

It was raining again, and some shops had already taken down their Christmas decorations. Window dressers were sticking up sales notices. Someone had thrown a deflated Santa Claus into the bushes at the side of the road and the plastic flapped, wet and forlorn, against the pavement.

Inside the pub was still bright and cheerful, though. Fairy lights twisted around the bar, and foil bells and one-dimensional reindeer were stuck on the walls. It wasn't busy yet. Just two couples and one old codger on his own in a corner when they first walked in. But there were several rooms. Stella led the way, glancing back and forth until she spotted a middle-aged bloke on his own at a corner table. She nodded at Jordan.

"I'll get you a drink. That way, we won't have to buy him one," Jordan said as he turned to walk to the bar.

It was petty, but Stella grinned and gave a thumbs-up.

The service was quick, and Jordan crossed the pub with two half-pints of lager.

Carl looked up in surprise as he joined them at the table. "Who's this?" he said.

"A friend."

"What we have to discuss is private, like, isn't it?"

"What do you think we are going to discuss, Carl?" Stella said.

"Well, my money, like."

"Your money?" Stella raised her eyebrows.

"Yeah, the money your uncle is getting from you for me. Though, actually, maybe I'm re-thinking that under the circumstances. Maybe I'll have another word with Geoff. Now we've met up you could just give it straight to me."

Jordan hadn't spoken. He sipped at his drink, fiddled with his phone, and gazed around the room.

Stella took a gulp of her drink and drew in a breath. "There is no money, Carl. Never will be for you. I don't know why you think I would consider having anything to do with you and your business practices. Christ, you know I'm a police officer. I don't understand why you would go this route. It stops here. You leave my uncle Geoff alone and you keep away from me."

He nodded and glanced back and forth between Jordan and Stella. "First of all, you need to remember that I didn't approach you. You asked for this meet. Second, your uncle owes me from way back. I don't know what problems you have between you two, but if you won't help him out, that's your affair. It's bloody stingy, I reckon. You're rolling in it, minted, and you can't help your own family out. But if that's the way it is, so be it." He shrugged. "Tell Geoff I'll be in touch, and we'll sort something different." He put his hand on his phone, resting on the tabletop, and began to push his chair back. He was obviously intent on leaving.

Jordan reached out to lay his hand on top of Carl's. With the other hand, he took out his warrant card. "We've had a look at your record, mate. We're watching you. I don't know what you think Stella or her uncle owes you, but it ends here. Crawl back under your rock and leave decent people to get on with their lives."

Carl dragged his hand out from under Jordan's palm. "Decent people. Really? Shows how much you know. This is not over. Not at all, and don't think waving your wallet scared me. This is my country." He made a show of wiping his hand on his trousers. "Bloody Bounty bar."

"Is that the best you can do?" Jordan said. "I haven't heard that one for years." He was tempted to point out the misuse of the insult but in the end, it didn't matter, and he didn't see any point trying to deal with such ignorance.

Carl sneered down at them, turned and stomped out of the pub.

They watched through the window as he slid into an ageing Discovery and rumbled out of the car park.

Chapter 39

In the car park, they agreed Stella would get her uncle Geoff into the station. "If I bring him in, it'll put him on edge. I'll make out I'm too busy to meet him anywhere else. I need to know just what that insect has over him. Frankly, it's a worry. Not about Geoff. Whatever he's done was his own bloody fault. But I need to protect Granda, if I can." She clenched her fists and tutted. "Bloody families, eh? You can't live with 'em and da de dah."

Jordan touched her shoulder. "We'll sort it out. Really, do you think it can be something so bad? You know your uncle, could he have done something really dodgy, or is this plonker just flexing his not-very-impressive mental muscles?"

"Frankly, I don't know. They've known each other for a long time and there's been stuff in the past that everyone glossed over. I told you about the time the older ones were on edge. When the car showroom burned. Nobody ever explained what that was all about. It's never mentioned."

"I reckon you should do it soon. Try for tomorrow if you can." Then, Jordan told her about the phone call from John. "That's niggling at me. Obviously, this Tony Yates was lying right from the start. I'm going over everything he said because I think there is something there that's important. Tomorrow I'm going back to speak to old Frank. I want to keep in touch with him, anyway. I'd like to get him to accept help or at least organise for him to get food regularly. He doesn't mind a natter, and there might be something there that he doesn't realise is important."

"If he doesn't want to have meals on wheels, why not see if you can help him sort regular deliveries from the supermarket? At least that way he'd get bread and basics to feed him. Is it really not a question of money, or was he just being proud?" Stella said.

"Difficult to tell. I have to step carefully. You know what these old folk can be like."

"Don't I just," Stella said, and Jordan knew she was thinking about her granddad. He laid his hand on her shoulder again and gave it a squeeze. She smiled up at him and turned away to plip the key to unlock her car. She nodded and squared her shoulders as she walked across the car park.

* * *

It was great to get home to the smell of dinner cooking and the sound of quiet jazz coming from the sound system.

Penny brought him wine and took his coat. "You're a bit late, love."

"I was at the pub with Stella." He grinned, winding her up.

She turned away to hang his overcoat on the hook and when she turned back, the look on her face jolted him.

"Hey, I was joking. I was at the pub with Stella, that's true, but it was work." He pulled her closer, and she wrapped her arms around him.

"I'm being silly," she said. "We missed you so much over Christmas and then I found who you'd spent it with. I like Stella. I really do but..."

Jordan buried his face in the cloud of dark hair and hugged her tightly. "There is nothing you have to worry about. I'll admit the stupid sods in work are always looking for gossip, and Stella and I are aware of it. Okay, now and then I'm tempted to egg them on a bit. I don't, though, it's not worth it. But on my Nana's life, Penny, you must never worry. There is only you. You and Harry. Tell me you know that." He pushed her back so that he could look into her eyes.

She closed her eyes for a moment and then nodded. "Just feeling a bit emotional, sorry."

"Come on, the smell of that roast is making me hungry and I need to pick your brain about food deliveries for pensioners."

Chapter 40

Frank Dirkin was staggering around his kitchen wearing a heavy wool dressing gown, steadying himself with a stick and the backs of chairs. There was the offer of tea and toast. Jordan took the drink and turned down the food. Who knew how much bread the old man had left? He had brought a box of tea bags, though. "We don't like this brand. Penny brought them back from London. One of the cousins had got a pile of them. Didn't ask where from. Better not to know sometimes. Don't think they're hinky, but well…"

The old man laughed. "What you don't know can't hurt you, eh?"

"I wish that was true, Frank. In my work, what you don't know is often the very thing that does the most harm."

"Aye. I can see that. You no nearer to finding out what happened to them across the road?"

"Some things are becoming clearer, I guess. We know they'd cancelled their carers and we reckon they'd taken on someone else. Haven't found out who yet."

"And the van?"

Jordan shook his head. "Nothing certain. There is one round at that empty house, as you said. I took a picture. Could you say whether this was the one?"

Frank fished his glasses out of the dressing gown pocket and squinted down at the screen. "I don't remember all that colour on the side. It's the right sort. I like them VWs. Okay, they're German, but we've let bygones be bygones and they make good cars. Like I say, I don't think so but it could be. Maybe they painted it."

"Did you know the woman who lived there? She's dead now."

Frank shook his head. "Too far round. Funny how you know the ones nearby but, unless you work with them, travel on the same train or whatever, you don't often know the ones further away. I expect it's different if you have kids. You see folk at the school gate, don't you? But we never had none."

"Seems as though she was related to Tony Yates, the bloke from the corner house."

"Oh, aye. Can't say as I knew him, neither. Didn't like what I saw of him. Used to have dodgy blokes coming round. You know the type, flash cars and leather jackets. Now I come to think of it, though…"

"Yes?"

"One of them had a van. Now, that was a plain one. I never thought of that, perhaps I've caught that Alzheimer's. Don't think that helps much. Haven't seen him for a bit."

"I don't think there's anything wrong with your memory, Frank. Could you describe the bloke that had the van? How long ago did you see him?"

"Oh, it's a bit since, perhaps six months. Like I say, a bit rough looking. Another one with a shaved head. I know it's the fashion now, but it makes 'em all look like thugs. Not as tall as you. White, thick set, no beard." The old man closed his eyes. "Nearly always wore a leather coat if it were cold. Not a jacket. It were longer than that."

"Ha. As I say, nothing wrong with your memory, Frank."

The comment drew a smile on the wrinkly face.

Jordan spent a few minutes trying to persuade the other man to look at a brochure about meal deliveries.

"I said as I didn't want them meals on wheels."

"No. This is different. They're nothing to do with the council. You order the food over the phone. Whole meals, big or small, just what you want and they bring them for you to keep in the freezer. They're reasonably priced. Have a look. If you like the sound of it, I can always help you set up your account. My wife works for the Citizens Advice. Lots of the people she talks to find these are a godsend."

"I'll have a look. Later on."

Jordan's phone rang, and he used the interruption as an excuse to leave. He was already over half an hour late. It was true he had been working and there was useful information, but he needed to move.

He returned the call on the hands-free as he drove away.

"I'm on the way in, Vi. Is there news?"

"Yep. It might be something interesting. Can't tell yet. There's more information about the woman we assume was Tony Yates's mother."

"I won't be long, and I've just thought of something. Should be with you soon." He stopped briefly outside the empty house and took a couple of pictures with his mobile phone camera. He walked down the side of the van with his Swiss Army knife in his hand. Kneeling just behind the passenger door, he poked and pried and, after just a minute, he smiled at his work.

Chapter 41

They might not have been completely back to full strength, but the station felt relatively normal. Jordan glanced at the big room on the way to his office to dump his bag and coat. Kath was away from her desk and standing by his door before there was time to turn on his computer.

"Right, let's see what you've got," Jordan said.

"The house belonged to Tony Yates's mother. I've confirmed he was the same Tony Yates who lives opposite our crime scene. There are no other relatives so, presumably, the house will now belong to him. The sale prices recently have been round about two hundred and fifty thousand. That means it won't be liable for inheritance tax, so it's probably not in the hands of a solicitor and he's doing the probate himself. Unless she had loads of money as well."

"Always possible," Jordan said.

"But, I think not. This is where it all gets more interesting. She was ill for quite a time before she died. I know this from comments in the announcements on the *Echo* website and his Facebook page. He hasn't posted lately by the way, I checked. She had cancer and everyone agreed in the end that her death was a relief. I contacted the council this morning, and she had carers for a good while. Pension credit entitled her to several other grants and aids, including attendance allowance. So, the local authority paid towards her care. Then, about six months before she died, the family cancelled them. She was still claiming the money she was entitled to, but no carers or nurses. That rang some bells for me. Isn't that just what the Lipscowes did?"

"Sounds very much like it."

"It doesn't make sense. She wasn't in hospital. I had a word with the receptionist at her doctor's and she was very helpful. She remembered Mrs Yates and was more than happy to talk about her. She died at home."

"Was there a post-mortem?"

"No, she'd been ill and her death was expected."

One of the civilian clerks was hovering in the background, a piece of paper in his hand.

"Yeah, Darren, isn't it? Can I help you?" Jordan said.

"This might be nothing, Detective Inspector, but I've just been looking at the PNC reports that came in over the holiday. There was a double suspicious death. Over in New Brighton. It was an elderly couple. She was suffocated, and he cut his wrists. It was only discovered when a neighbour knocked on Boxing Day. She'd invited them for drinks, but they didn't turn up. Thing is, the initial thoughts were a suicide and murder. As I say, it might be nothing, but you never know."

"Get me the details. I want the address and the name of the SIO for that. Well done," Jordan said. "Okay, heads up," he said to the room in general. "I need you to find me Tony Yates. He came back into the country on Christmas Eve. He was on foot from the Eurostar. Kath, can you lift some pictures from his Facebook page?"

"Yeah, there's plenty that I can use to know what he looks like."

"Great. See if you can work your magic on the cameras. It's a hell of a long shot, I realise that, but I really would love to know where he got himself off to." Jordan picked up the phone.

John Grice answered on the second ring.

"How are you, John?" he asked.

"Not bad. I'm still testing positive, though. Is there something I can do?"

"Yeah. I'm sending the details of two suspicious deaths over the holidays. Contact the SIO and get all you can. We need to know specifically about carers. Did she have them? Where were they from? Had she changed them lately?"

"On it, boss."

Stella knocked on the door frame. "Uncle Geoff is coming in, boss. About an hour."

"Have you told him what it's about?"

"Sort of. I told him I needed a word and couldn't get away. I said it was about the money, but that's as far as I went."

"Right. Let's bring him in here. It's cramped, but better than an interview room."

There hadn't been a free moment since he'd stepped into the office, but there was a vibe that he liked. Things were moving. It wasn't even clear yet which direction they were taking, but just moving was good.

Chapter 42

Geoff May was a small man. Barely five foot six. His mousy-coloured hair was receding and though he didn't sport a comb-over, he constantly smoothed and arranged it. Jordan watched him glance in the office window, checking his appearance. He was dressed in jeans and a sweatshirt with a short fur-lined jacket over. He dragged this off and laid it carefully in the corner of the room. Smiling, he shook Jordan's hand.

"Nice to meet you, Jordan. Our Stel is always going on about you. It's nice finally to put a face to the name."

Jordan nodded and pulled his chair to the corner of his desk. Less formal, but not quite friendly.

Stella closed the door and leaned against it.

Geoff glanced between them. "Not sure what's going on here. I thought we were just going to have a quick chat, our Stel."

"We are, Uncle Geoff. But I wanted the DI to be in on it."

Geoff frowned across at her. She told him in brief about the meeting in the Black Bull. He looked back and forth between them and swallowed hard. He scratched the side of his face.

"I wish you hadn't done that, love," he said. "There was no need. You could just have said no and left it at that."

"You know I did, Geoff. I said no several times, and it didn't make you stop. Now, that made me suspicious. I had a chat with DI Carr here and he agreed there was something not quite right about it all."

"You daft bitch. What do you want to go involving other people in our private business for?"

Jordan slid to the edge of his seat. "I think you should watch your language there, Geoff. Maybe think about where you are right now."

The other man stood and reached for his jacket. "Okay, I'm out of here. You've screwed up, Stel. You really have. We're both going to regret this. Now, shift so I can get out."

"Just sit down, will you, Geoff?" Jordan said.

"No, I bloody won't."

Stella tried, Jordan tried, to calm him and bring him to a stage where they could ask him exactly what he was upset about. In the end, he marched to the door and pushed Stella aside. He strode past her and stomped across the big room. From the window, they watched him cross the car park. He stalled the car twice before pulling out of the parking space and swerving onto the main road.

"Right," Jordan said. "That was quite a reaction. Sorry, Stella, but that wasn't normal. What do you want to do next? I don't think he'll be asking for more money. You could just let it go now. If you decide to do that, I'll respect your decision. Frankly, though, he looked to me like a man with bigger problems than his niece washing his dirty linen in public."

"You're right, boss. I will say his behaviour shocked me. But what the hell am I going to do now?"

Chapter 43

Vi came to the office door. "Everything okay?"

"Fine." Stella slid past her and went to sit at her desk.

Vi turned and frowned as she saw her snatch a tissue from the box beside her computer and dab at her eyes.

"Anything I can do, boss?" Vi said.

"No, it's personal. Best leave her for now. I'm helping her to sort it. Was there something?"

"That house was Tony Yates's mother's address. That's not where the car is registered, though. It's the flower shop, the one on the side decals. No record that I can find of his mum having anything to do with a shop of any sort, or Tony himself come to that. The flower shop is in a woman's name, as is the insurance. Kylie Heywood. I'm going to research her now, obviously, but I thought I'd keep you up to date."

The knots and tangles were becoming more and more puzzling. They had a lot of information, but fitting it together was the challenge.

Jordan took a couple of sheets of paper from the copier. He drew a circle with spokes and put the Lipscowes in the middle. The sighting on the bridge was at the end of one spoke. He was convinced that the witnesses had seen poor Stanley being dragged to his death. Another spoke had the carer, both the change in provider and the suspicious visits late in the night. Alongside that, he noted the money from Stanley's bank account. There were very few reasons for cash withdrawals these days, especially for such quantities and with nothing to show for it.

There was something else he needed to clarify. He picked up the phone and rang Vickie. "I don't mean to hassle you, but I reckon this could be important."

"No probs, Jordan. I think I've got that here somewhere. I was just trying to catch up after the break. Okay, here we are."

The presents under the tree had been unremarkable. Soft clothes, lotions, and bath products. A small necklace of red beads. These had been for Tracy. There had been just one wrapped present for Stanley. "I have to say, this is peculiar," Vickie said. "Not the sort of present I would have expected."

"Okay, you've got my attention," Jordan said.

"There was a gold ring. I believe it was her wedding ring. I checked, and she wasn't wearing one when they brought her body away from the crime scene. It certainly wasn't new. There was wear on the edges. That was in a box, with one of those little key rings with two-part hearts."

"Sorry, don't know what you mean."

"Course you do. You get two in the set, and they fit together, two parts of the heart that make a whole one. Now, that was new, but I've checked thoroughly, and the other half wasn't there. Not in any of the stuff brought from the house. She had a keyring in her handbag, but it was a fluffy ball. Possibly easy for her to grab hold of."

"She knew, didn't she? She knew he was cheating on her. It would have been really difficult for her to leave him. Being ill as she was. But she wanted to let him know. God, that's so bloody horrible. The poor woman," Jordan said.

"If he'd opened it, I would have thought it could point to him being the one who killed her", said Vickie. "You know, some reaction, maybe a row, maybe guilt. But it was wrapped. It had a bow tied round it and no evidence anyone had tampered with it."

Jordan drew another spoke on his wheel – marriage breakdown – and ended the call.

There was plenty of activity in the incident room and when he reported to DCI Josh Lewis the next day, he'd be able to demonstrate they were following plenty of leads. He'd just need to blur the edges a bit regarding outcomes and hypotheses.

Stella had calmed down and was busy helping with the search for the white VW; she managed a watery smile as he passed her desk on the way to the coffee machine. "I'm going to send you an address," she said. "Can you add it to the list of things to search for? It shouldn't take you long."

"Come round to my place tonight. We'll talk." Jordan hoped that if he showed Penny that all was normal between them, it would settle any lingering worries she had. "Make it about half seven, that'll give us chance to get Harry settled."

Chapter 44

Jordan was on his way home when the phone rang. He was relieved to see it was John's number. At least he was unlikely to bring more drama being out of the office.

"Boss, sorry to bother you, but I reckon you'd want to know about this."

"Okay, go ahead."

"I've had a long chat with the detective sergeant in New Brighton. The victims there, Joan and Peter Lester, had been dead about twenty-four hours when the woman next door found them. That puts it on Christmas Eve or Christmas Day. It's early days so they still have scene-of-crime people in there doing their thing. According to the neighbour, they didn't have carers. They both had health problems, so they had a cleaner who came twice a week." He paused. "She usually drove a small, dark-coloured car.

On Christmas Eve, the neighbour was waiting for a last-minute delivery and was alerted when a white van drew up outside. She watched out of the window, and saw a couple going into the Lesters' house. They went down the side passage, and she assumed they must be friends or family visiting. She's given a description. It's not too detailed. It was dark and whatnot. But he had a bald head. She mentioned that, particularly. A big bloke, she said. This is the clincher for me. They had assumed a murder-suicide, but they rushed through the post-mortem exam as soon as they could after the holiday. The medical examiner isn't happy. Apparently, the angle of the cuts on the bloke's arms don't suggest he did it himself. And there's no way the woman did it and then suffocated herself, is there?"

"Okay. Well, that is very interesting. Damn, I wish I could send you over there."

"I've arranged a Zoom meeting with the SIO. Do you want me to send you the code for that? It'll be tomorrow morning. They have an operational name, by the way. I wondered if it should be part of Song Thrush, but apparently not. It's Rushmore. Apparently, that's a mountain somewhere in America. Seems odd, but that's what we have."

"Okay. Send me the access details for the Zoom. Great work, John."

He was waiting at the traffic lights at Switch Island. He clicked off his left-hand indicator and pulled the nose of his car into the middle lane. There was the blast of a horn behind him, and he raised a hand in apology.

If he'd been asked, it would be difficult to explain what had taken him to Aintree and the estate where the Lipscowes' house was, what drew him down Keble Drive, and why he was unsurprised to find that the white van had gone. He thumped his hand hard on the steering wheel and swore aloud. He had known this was a risk, but also that he hadn't had enough manpower to put it under surveillance.

Chapter 45

Now there was reason enough to set up an all-ports alert and notify forces nationwide to watch for the van. They had the registration. It could be that Tony Yates would be picked up with it, but that might be a bit of a leap. Jordan reckoned they were due for a big break, though. The excitement was tempered by the knowledge that another couple had died while they were investigating. There would be questions to answer if the two turned out to be connected. Jordan spent the time before Stella arrived making sure that his book was up to date and any investigation would find that there had been nothing further he could have done. Jordan rang the DCI to let him know about the developing situation. There was no response. He tried several times. It would have to wait. He'd deal with any fallout later.

He paced a little.

"You know there's nothing you can do now. You can't go out there looking for it yourself. Let the system do its work," Penny told him.

Stella was already fully aware of what was going on when she arrived and the atmosphere was edged with impatience. She accepted a small shandy and Jordan stuck to sparkling water.

"They might not find him tonight, boss," Stella said.

Jordan nodded and glanced at his watch. ANPR, announcements at roll call, notifications on the Airwave network. If the car was out on the road, they would find it. It was essential they find it quickly. Just in case. They needed every chance to search it for trace evidence from the couple's house.

The knife that had cut Peter Lester was in the bathroom, along with his body. There were fingerprints, but they matched the old man's. Every contact left something and now they had reason to ask for DNA and fingerprints from Tony Yates and whoever the woman with him was. The lies he had told gave them reason to bring him in for questioning and all that meant. But they had to find him first.

They had a snack. They tried hard with the conversation. Penny was relaxed, and there didn't seem to be any residual awkwardness. They discussed Christmas; it cleared the air, everything out in the open. That led inexorably to the problem of Uncle Geoff.

Stella told Penny about the problem, knowing that she would keep it to herself. After all, she must have heard many other family problems in her work with the Citizens Advice service.

This time, Penny had very little new to contribute. "You've got to speak to your uncle. Find out what this Carl person is holding over him. It might well be less serious than he thinks. But if he doesn't tell you, there's nothing you can do."

Stella knew this was true and Jordan had simply been waiting for her to acknowledge it. "Will you come with me?" she asked. "When we have a chance. We'll go to his flat and force him to tell us. Maybe Penny's right. It might be nothing and he's just scared of Carl. He was always a bit in awe of him from what my mum said. Perhaps this is all leftover bullying from when they were kids."

Jordan nodded, and Stella breathed a huge sigh.

The phone rang and the two women watched as Jordan gave monosyllabic responses and asked for information.

"Okay. Police on the Wirral stopped the van on the A55 heading to Wales. They're taking it to New Brighton and we can go over there and sit in on the interview."

"Great! So, tomorrow?" Stella said.

"Oh yes, no time tonight."

Penny brought out two more glasses and poured the Côtes-du-Rhône that she'd opened for herself.

"No need to hold back then," she said. "Things look better now." She smiled at her husband. "Oh, but... I know that look. There's something else."

There was indeed something else. The white van was the one parked in Aintree. Very little doubt about that. The number matched and it was the one they were relying on to link the two cases.

The something else was the driver. An IC1 female. They had a brief description. She was small, late twenties or early thirties, with dark hair and blue eyes. She had refused to give her name and had no ID, not even a driving licence.

Chapter 46

Jordan called John first thing to let him know there wouldn't be a Zoom because he was on his way to New Brighton. "I'm not upstaging you here, John, but I reckon it's worth us going over there now."

"It's okay, boss. Things have changed, I get that. I'm off to the doctor this morning, anyway. I can't shift this cough. Good news is that I'm testing negative now. If he gives me the all-clear, I'll be in work later today."

"Take the day, John. We need you, but we need you well and Stella and I are going to be over on the Wirral for a lot of it. When you have a chance, can you research a retail address? I gave it to Stella yesterday, but she didn't get to it. I've sent it on in an email."

* * *

Detective Sergeant Andy Campbell met Stella and Jordan just inside the sliding black metal gates at the Wirral Custody Suite. It was another cold, damp day, and they didn't hang around for long in the car park. Inside, the staff gave them coffee. It wasn't bad. It was warm and sweet, but Jordan really wished he'd brought his flask in from the car. Then again, it would have been rude, and he could look forward to it on the way back to Liverpool. The night before had turned into a bit of a session. Stella stayed over and they had both quietly swallowed paracetamol and drunk water on the trip under the tunnel.

Campbell reassured them they had offered the woman, who had given her name as Shandy Price, food when she arrived, and again in the morning. She wouldn't eat, though she had drunk tea. They had explained her rights, showed her the written notice, and made sure she could read. She hadn't asked for legal representation, and hadn't wanted anyone informed of her whereabouts.

The white van was being kept at Birkenhead Police Station. Everyone knew it was to be processed as a potential crime scene. They were sharing information and had invited Vickie Frost to send someone to help, but she'd chosen to come herself. It was reassuring and satisfying to have proper co-operation.

"We're holding her on suspicion of being involved in a crime. That's all we've got right now," said Campbell. "She hasn't given us much of a response. In fact, she hardly said a word. We're not absolutely convinced the name's genuine. Mind, we're still looking. With no date of birth, no place, no next of kin, it's a long job. It might look as though we've been dragging our heels, but it was late last night when she arrived, so we're still researching this morning. She had nothing on her person. Some sweets in her pocket and that was it. There might be stuff in the van. They'll let us know if they find anything." The sergeant took a deep breath and leaned forward. He lowered his voice. "Okay, cards on the table, Detective Inspector. This is my first murder. I've only just transferred to major cases and I really don't want to screw it up. We've been sticking to the book."

"You're doing the right thing, mate. We'll help as much as we can. How long has she been in custody?" Jordan asked.

Campbell glanced at the clock on the wall. "Nine hours."

"Time's getting on then."

"It is, but we thought you'd want us to wait for you before we interviewed her fully."

"I appreciate that, but we should get on with it."

The building wasn't as old as many police stations, and it was still clean and warm. It wasn't exactly welcoming, but that wasn't the aim. The interview room was an echo of so many others. Plain and functional, nothing more.

Stella and Jordan sat beside the table and Campbell brought another chair in to join them. After Shandy shuffled in – head down, shoulders hunched – and slid onto the other chair with a sigh, they went through the routine with the recording apparatus.

Jordan turned and glanced at Stella, who gave a brief nod. Although it would normally be the responsibility of the local officer to lead the interview, Campbell had happily handed the job over. "I had a go last night. Got absolutely nowhere with her," he had said. "Maybe a more senior officer will get through to her. It'll make her see how serious we are. If that doesn't work, we can let your sergeant have a go. Woman to woman and all that." The smile he had directed at Stella was probably intended to take any sting out of the idea that she was a last resort. She'd decided to give him the benefit of the doubt, at least.

"Do you want anything?" Jordan asked.

Shandy shook her head.

"We need a word with you about the van you were driving yesterday when the police stopped you."

The young woman chewed at her lip and raised a finger to wipe it under her nose. Stella took a pack of tissues from her pocket and offered one across the table. Shandy glanced up and reached for the paper handkerchief.

"Ta."

She wiped her eyes and nose and began to shred the thin paper to bits upon the tabletop.

"Is it your van, Shandy?" Jordan asked.

There was no response. "We need to know whom it belongs to. We think someone used it in a crime. If that's the case, then obviously we're going to think it must have been you. You see that, don't you?"

There was no response.

"Did someone ask you to drive the van, Shandy?" Jordan asked.

No response.

"You're not helping yourself here. We just need you to answer our questions, that's all."

Somewhere else in the building, there was a high-pitched scream. A door slammed and there was the sound of running feet. Campbell scratched at his cheek, unmoved. Jordan glanced at the door. The uniformed officer standing beside the wall raised his eyebrows and left at a non-verbal granting of permission from Campbell.

The noise continued, more screaming, shouting and running. They never found out what it was, just another event in the day of the custody suite, but it loosened Shandy's tongue. For what it was worth.

Chapter 47

She frowned at the door, and they saw her throat move with a nervous gulp. When she spoke, it was just above a whisper. "Bought it, didn't I?"

They waited, nothing followed.

"Who did you buy it from?" Jordan asked.

"Internet."

"Do you have the name?" Jordan said.

"Just a site that sells stuff."

"No, I mean the name of the person you bought it from."

"No."

"You bought a van from someone without knowing their name?" Jordan pulled a file from his briefcase. "Was it this bloke?" He showed her a picture of Tony Yates.

"Dunno."

"Just have a proper look and maybe you'll have a better idea." He slid the paper across the table so that she had to see it.

The glance she gave him was the first sign of a stronger reaction, and it wasn't friendly. "Said I don't know. Didn't meet him. Did it all online."

"How did you get the keys?"

"Post."

"He sent you the key to a valuable vehicle through the post."

"Yep."

"How much did you pay him?"

"Mind your own. That's my business." She stared at him now and sniffed.

"Everything is my business when I'm investigating a serious crime. So, how much did you pay? What do you know about the person who sold it and where is the paperwork?"

"Couple of thousand, deposit. Nothing. It's in the post. I want to go for a pee."

There was no choice. Although she may have shown little interest in the booking procedure, she obviously had taken it in and knew how to use it to her advantage.

"DS May will go with you."

"I can pee on my own."

"You can't when you're under investigation for a serious crime. You have to face the fact that you might not be doing anything on your own for a long, long time, Shandy."

She shrugged her shoulders, sneered at Jordan, and pushed her chair back.

"Before you go," Campbell said. "Which sales site was it?"

The response was a foregone conclusion.

"Can't remember."

"She's lying, of course," Jordan said. "That's probably enough to get permission to hold her for longer, but not enough to charge her with anything. Not yet."

Campbell's phone vibrated.

"They've found a handbag hidden in a toolbox in the back of the van. Your CSI sergeant has arrived. Do you want to go down and have a look?"

"No, let's stay here." Jordan called Vickie. "Can you send me a text with her name and any other personal details you can find? Quick as you can."

Stella stopped on the way back from the ladies and bought bottles of water for the room. Shandy had already opened hers and swigged from the top as she sat down.

"Bank details of the seller," Jordan said, as if there had been no interruption.

"Paid with PayPal straight to the site."

"Oh, come on, you did not." His phone vibrated. "So, Kylie, time you stopped with all the lies, I think."

Her head jerked up now at the sound of her real name. "Kylie Heywood, from Bootle. Tell us where Tony is."

She put down the water and slowly clapped her hands. "You found my bag. Wow."

"We found the bag. The technicians are pulling the van apart right now. They will find every hair, every fibre, and anything else – including blood – that there is. Since last night we have your fingerprints and your DNA and we have the fingerprints and DNA of two poor dead victims.

I'll leave it up to you to work out what happens if we find anything that makes us wonder just what you used the van for. Don't you think it would be good if you just told us where Tony is? Not fair that he's out there walking around and you're here, is it?"

"Who's Tony, anyway? Don't know no Tony, do I? I only just bought it. Wednesday. I'd never seen it before then. I don't know what happened to it before I got it. You'll never be able to make anyone take you seriously."

Jordan nodded, made a note in his notebook, and smiled at her.

"Do you make a habit of travelling abroad with people you don't know?" Jordan said.

Kylie made a show of puzzlement and confusion. It was fairly convincing. "Haven't a clue what you're talking about, mate."

Jordan pulled out the pictures of Tony at the airport. He laid out four of them on the table. He pointed to Kylie, standing near to him and accessing the check-in gate at the same time.

She shook her head.

"That is you. We know border control stamped your passport in and out as they did with this person." He pointed again at the pictures. "It's obvious to anyone that you were with him."

She pushed back into the chair and folded her arms. "Don't know. Haven't a clue."

* * *

"I think that's all I need for now, Detective Sergeant. Unless you have anything else."

"Nope, that's fine. No need to be formal, just call me Andy, if that's okay." Jordan smiled at the younger officer.

It wasn't until they were outside the room and Kylie was being walked back to her cell that Campbell asked his question. "I don't see why you stopped. She's right. We haven't got anything, really. If she didn't pick up the van

131

until Wednesday, she can't have had anything to do with the murders at Christmas."

"Okay," Jordan said. "I have some important information for you, and I thought we should let her stew for a bit."

"What information?"

"Is there anywhere we can get some decent coffee? And I'll fill you in on just what Kylie Heywood was getting up to before Christmas."

"Yeah, coffee. I've got a machine in my office." Campbell grinned broadly as he led the way. "So, she lied about everything?"

"She did. The next step is to encourage her to think about telling us the truth, and where Tony Yates has taken himself off to."

Vickie's name showed up on another incoming message. This one had an image attached. Jordan opened the file and gave a short 'huh' when he viewed the picture. "I need to get on to Liverpool; then why don't we forget the coffee and find somewhere to have lunch? I feel the need for chips. You must know of a good chippy round there, Andy."

"I do indeed. It's a short drive but well worth it, and you can sit and enjoy the view of the estuary and the birds."

Chapter 48

The rain held off. Jordan didn't want them to eat inside at the restaurant. It was a work meeting, and the place was too busy for them to talk comfortably without being overheard. Outside, the wind was icy, blowing all the way across the Irish sea. It was too cold for them to sit on the benches.

This was a popular spot; even out of season and in the dead time between Christmas and New Year, there were cars parked on The Parade at Parkgate. Walkers were striding out along the route overlooking the Dee Estuary. Wind rustled the reeds into endless green waves and turned the grey water choppy. It was lovely even now, and Jordan stored the place away as one to bring Penny and the boy.

They'd taken one of the pool cars, and DS Campbell found a parking spot just before the start of the double yellow lines.

"We'll eat in the car if you like," he said. "That way, we won't be overheard."

"It'll stink afterwards," Stella said.

Campbell grinned. "Yeah, it'll drive the next occupants potty."

The food was hot and delicious. The windows were steamy and streaming with condensation. Jordan cracked his open a little. It was close and confined but pleasant, sheltered from the weather, and they ate in silence for a while.

"We should really have ice cream afterwards. That's the usual tradition," Campbell said. "I reckon you'll want to give that a miss today, though."

"Yeah, a hot drink might go down better," Stella said.

"We'll have that coffee when we get back."

Jordan folded the polystyrene containers with the little wooden fork inside and took all three to the waste bin. Stella's pack of tissues came into its own again, along with hand sanitizer from her bag. Once they had cleaned up as much as they could, Jordan took out the airport pictures. "We've updated the all-ports alert now that we know Tony Yates won't be in that van. It makes things more difficult. He could well be in the wind already. But we need to keep going."

"So, should we assume she was going to join him?" Campbell said.

"Could very well be, I reckon."

"She was buggering off to Wales, wasn't she?" Stella asked.

"That was the direction she was heading in, but there're plenty of places between here and there. I don't reckon we're going to get much joy from just asking her, are we?" said Campbell.

"Not from the present showing," Jordan said. "We have to accept that we could be looking at letting her go, for the time being, at least."

"We'll keep the vehicle, though?"

Jordan shook his head. "Might be best to let it all go with no fuss."

"What?" Campbell turned in the driver's seat to stare at him.

"Vi just messaged us from Copy Lane," Stella said. "She went to the address on Kylie's driving licence. It's a flat in a converted house. Bit grot, apparently. I don't see her going back there, at least not for a while. She'll know we'll be watching it."

"But hasn't he got two houses in Aintree? Maybe he'll be there?"

Jordan shook his head. "I don't think that's the case. He lied about where he was going over Christmas. That was obviously to muddy the waters. We've got them under observation as much as we can. As for Kylie, she's lied about where she got the van."

"And everything else," Stella said.

"Let's face it, it's hard to find a way through all these lies and confusion. We could do with taking a breath. Get our board updated."

"So, you've no idea where he might be? And no idea where she might head to if we let her go," Campbell said.

Jordan had thought of all of this, but he had also acknowledged, if only to himself, that he had little to link Tony Yates to the actual killings. The lies were important, but there could be many reasons for them. The van, that was something else, and now they had Kylie, who was with him at the airport. They had the witness who saw a bald man in the van. His instinct told him they were connected, but instinct didn't stand up in court. Instinct didn't get him permission to search the property. He needed something to link the two, and then, he needed to prove they had been involved with the killings. It was all just a bit too tenuous for comfort.

"There is one possibility. Slim, but it's all we've got. If you're happy to let her go, we have an address. Apart from that, right now, we've nothing concrete to hold her on," Jordan said. "The witness mentioned a bald bloke – she could never be mistaken for that."

"Where is this address?" Campbell said.

"I've got a colleague checking on that right now. I believe it's a genuine option, but until I hear from John, we won't know for sure."

"He's sick, isn't he?" Stella said.

"He's better. Coming in tomorrow. This was a check on the web. We just need to know the place actually exists."

"You're being very mysterious."

"Sorry, Stel, I'm not meaning to be. I wanted confirmation before I said anything." He took out his phone and scrolled through the images in his gallery. "Here."

Stella leaned forward so that Campbell could see the screen, too.

"Oh, okay," Stella said. "So, John's checking it exists?"

"Yep."

Campbell rubbed a hand over his eyes. "God, I don't know. She's the only lead we've got for my dead couple, and if we lose contact with her, it could be a disaster. I'm not sure I want to risk it."

"We'll have to make sure that doesn't happen. But if we hold on to her for too long, it could be just as bad. We could limit our options," said Jordan. "I'd better explain. One of Vickie's technicians went to the house in Aintree.

He found this stuff" – he pointed to the picture – "partly burned in the back garden."

"What is that?" Campbell asked.

"Magnetic signage. It's vinyl. Taxis and suchlike use it when they need to use the cars without the adverts, because it's easy to take off. I saw it when it was on the van. It's the flower shop name. Look, at the moment we're just going round and round in the no-comment, don't-know, can't-remember cycle," Jordan said.

"Let's apply to have her bailed," Campbell said.

"If we do that, she's not going to be any further use to us. On bail, she'll just lie low. She might even go back to the grotty flat. She'll have time to plan. I don't think she'll risk leading us to Yates, but if we let her go, under the impression that we're stumped, it might lead somewhere. We've got this address. It's something. With luck, she doesn't realise we know about it. They don't know I saw the van in Aintree." He pointed at the phone again.

Campbell frowned and sucked his teeth as he pulled the car away from the kerb. "If you think it's best, then okay."

"Listen, if this all goes pear-shaped, I'll make sure you're in the clear," Jordan said. "I'm the superior officer here, when all's said and done."

"Oh well, in that case, I'll go along with it."

Chapter 49

Jordan dropped Stella and Campbell at the custody centre. "Have another go at her. There's nothing to lose. I'm going to have a word with Vickie and a look at the van myself."

The van was in the car park behind the police station in Birkenhead. "Not ideal," Vickie said. "I would have preferred it back at our place, but they said to wait. We've put a cover over it. Anyway, the bad news is that someone has given it a good clean. Stinks of bleach. We've done our best. There's no sign of anything untoward. No blood, we've looked with the black light. No semen either, but then it's hardly a campervan, is it? Not even a skinny mattress. There was a tarp in the back, a tool kit where she hid the handbag, and a couple of cardboard boxes. We've bagged and tagged them, but I'm taking it away if the SIO here will give me permission."

"I reckon he will. He's a bit out of his depth, but keen to clear this up."

"Up to now, the only thing we found was hair on the driver's seat. Long and black, but if you've got the driver in custody, you don't need that so much at the moment. I've got it in here, and we'll make sure the evidence chain is sound." She indicated a crate containing several plastic bags, sealed and signed with the time and location. "Oh, she's not a short-haired blond, is she?"

Jordan laughed. "No. Was there anything else?"

"An ancient fag end stuck in a corner, damp and disgusting. There was some mud. I've taken samples of that; they're in the crate. Oh yeah, and a couple of petals under the driver's seat. Roses, possibly, but they were dried out and crinkly."

"Excellent."

She grinned at him. "Oh good. Glad you're happy. I prefer mine in bunches with a ribbon on."

"I'll bear that in mind."

"See you do. Shall I liaise about sending this van across the water?"

"No. I think the plan is going to be letting it go."

"What!?"

"Don't look at me like that. I know what I'm doing. I hope I do, anyway. I'm sticking my neck right out, so please try to look less as though you think I've got a zip up the back of my head."

"Jeez. Don't know what you're up to, Jordie, but you go for it, mate. I can get off back home then, eh?"

"Could you hang around for a bit? With luck, I'll have some more for you before the end of the day."

"Tell you what. I'm starving. Sub me for a meal, well, me and my two techs, and you're on."

"Done."

Chapter 50

It was very tempting to call John immediately after leaving Vickie and her techs discussing where to have their delayed meal. Jordan glared at the screen on his phone, willing it to ring. When it did light up and burble from the holder on the dashboard, he had clicked the answer button on his steering wheel before the first chime finished.

"John. What have you got?"

"First of all, yes, that address exists. The not-so-good news is that it closed down a while ago. I had a gander on Google Earth and it still showed the shop front with the same name as that which used to be on the removable signage on the side of the van. Blooms 'n' Bunches. But even then, two years ago, it looks empty. Nothing in the window and no buckets of flowers outside, or any of that palaver."

"Okay. Did you find the owner's name?"

"I did. Edward Heap. He's a developer, and he leases the block of shops. There's a little supermarket, one of those local-type ones. A card shop, chemist, a hairdresser, a takeaway, and the empty flower shop. The other places were working when Google recorded the image in 2020."

"Send me the address. That's brilliant, John. Just what I wanted to hear. Are you coming in tomorrow?"

"Yeah, the quack wanted to sign me off for another week, but I'm going doolally sitting at home and Da trying to make me eat soup."

"Excellent. See you then. In the meantime, see if you can contact this Mr Heap and find out if the rent is still being paid, and if so, by whom. Any information will be useful."

Back at the custody suite, Jordan stood in a small office with a viewing window alongside the interview room. He watched as Stella and Campbell struggled against the constant 'no comment' responses from Kylie Heywood.

There was a young cadet in the room with him. She admitted she was hoping to learn something from watching the interview. "It hasn't been very informative up to now. She's told them nothing. It's not for the want of trying, but she's immovable."

"Has she not asked for a solicitor?"

"Not while I've been here."

"Well, she can't have done then, can she?"

"Oh no, course not. They would have had to stop."

"There you go. You did learn something." Jordan delivered the comment with a smile and received a blushing, shy one in return.

He texted Stella.

Wind it up. We can let her go.

He was in the corridor when Kylie Heywood stormed from the room. She glared at him and promised lawyers and enquiries and rolling heads. He nodded at her and watched her stomp away.

"I hope this isn't going to come back and bite us on the bum," Stella said.

"You and me both. But what did we have? Nothing to charge her with, except she was driving a white van which could have been involved in a crime?"

"You know that's not all of it, though, boss."

"No, but I want Tony Yates and I want her to lead us to him."

"Shit," Campbell said, looking decidedly worried.

"Come on, Stel. I want to be out there when she picks up the van. I've asked Vickie to have it ready, so we won't have long."

"So, we are going to follow her, boss?"

"We are, but we know where she's going, anyway."

"I bloody hope so," Campbell said.

Chapter 51

The rush hour was over as Kylie pulled into the road outside the police station in Birkenhead. She turned right, passing the end of the side road where Jordan was waiting in his Golf. Behind him, Campbell was in the pool car.

They headed up Chester Street, where it split for the Queensway Tunnel. The traffic emerging from the tunnel was less than it would have been just an hour before.

They passed the whisky brewery, and there on the left was Cammell Laird.

"That's the shipyard, yeah?" Jordan said to Stella.

"Aye, still going. Not what it was, but doing okay, I think."

"Ever been in?"

"How do you mean, in?"

"To see the ships. To see the launches?"

"Oh, no. Never knew no one to get us an invite. Here they launch them stern first. Not like places where they have to put them in sideways. The Mersey's a proper river. Imagine building a shipyard where the river's not wide enough."

"You're a Scouser to your bones, aren't you? Nothing better than Liverpool."

"I am and nothing wrong with that," said Stella. "Okay, according to the map it's not far now. It's a right turn. There's a filling station on the corner."

As she stared at the little map, her phone rang. "Sorry, boss, is it okay?"

"Go for it."

There was little in the way of conversation and the DS sighed heavily as she clicked the 'off' button.

"Everything alright?" Jordan asked.

"No, I don't think so. But we're doing this right now, so one thing at a time."

Kylie had driven into the narrow road behind the shop. Jordan didn't follow. They would have been too obvious. He drove past and then stopped. Stella was out of the car almost before it had come to a complete halt. She peered around the corner as Jordan opened his door.

"No," she called, flapping her hand and running back to send him back into the driving seat. She made a gesture towards Campbell, her hand describing frantic circles as she threw herself back inside.

"What's going on?" Jordan said.

"She didn't stop. Slowed down a bit and then straight out at the other end. I reckon she's back on the main road." She twisted in the seat as she spoke. "Bloody hell, there she goes. Back the way we came."

The road was too narrow for an elegant three-point turn and Jordan mounted the pavement at both sides. Campbell was nearer to the back access road. He swerved into the narrow alley, and they heard him speeding past the storage garages.

"Let him know which way she's gone," Jordan said.

Stella sent a text.

As they pulled back onto the main road, Campbell flashed his headlights.

"Christ," Jordan said, "tell him to stop attracting attention. She's just ahead and slowing down. This is a development."

"Odd. Why go up there if he's not waiting for her?" Stella said.

"Good question. Okay, she's heading for the pub. Must have been a change of plan." He drove past and pulled into the kerb.

Stella waved at Campbell to carry on and park beyond them.

It was a large, chain-hotel pub and restaurant; the smell of hot fat and burned meat drifted towards them as they crossed the car park on foot. Jordan peered through the small panes into the dim interior. Kylie Heywood stood near the bar. One foot tapped impatiently on the floor as she waited to be served.

"We going in, or what?" Campbell asked.

Jordan held up a hand. "Hold on a minute. She's meeting someone. He's there." The others leaned closer to the window.

"Ah," Stella said.

"What, what?" Campbell was puffing with impatience.

Jordan took a step backwards. "That bloke is not Tony Yates."

Chapter 52

DS Campbell leaned forward. His breath steamed against the small pane. "That's not him? Are you sure? He's bald and big."

"I'm sure," Jordan said. "I had a couple of meetings with Tony Yates, and that's not him."

"So, it's the bald bloke from your murder, possibly. We made an assumption. We should know better." As Stella spoke, they stepped back into the car park.

"So, what do we do now?" Campbell asked.

"We can take stock. You could go in there and bring them both in on the strength of the sighting of the van and the identification given by your witness. I reckon you've got enough for 'the suspicion of'. The trouble is that if you do that, it leaves us out on a limb. The old bloke in Aintree mentioned that Tony Yates had friends with shaved heads, but that's pretty vague. I think it's up to you."

"Shit, I'm confused now. If this isn't Tony Yates, where is he? Does this mean that he's had nothing to do with your murder and therefore nothing to do with mine? In that case, I'm best off taking these two in."

Campbell pulled his Airwaves set from his pocket. "I'll call for backup."

Stella took in a breath. "Before you do that, and it has to be your choice, what about the flower shop? What's the connection with all of this?"

Campbell lowered his hand. "The van had the logo of Bloom 'n' Bunches. But then, the place isn't trading anymore, so they could have bought it second-hand."

"If that's the case, why are they here now? Why did Kylie head down that way?" Jordan said.

"Good point. Perhaps it's just a sort of meeting point."

"For what?" Stella said. "What are they actually doing? Why have they killed that old couple, maybe even two? If that's indeed what we're looking at here. It's all wide open."

"Maybe they didn't have anything to do with your murder," said Campbell.

Jordan and Stella could tell as he spoke that Campbell didn't believe his own words.

Jordan listened to the back and forth before he said, "They look as though they're settled for a while. Why not get a patrol car to come and keep an eye on things here, and we go back to the flower shop? I would like a look at that place. My instinct tells me it's more important than just the business that used to own the van. That doesn't gel with me."

"Give me a minute. Let me see if there's someone available," Campbell said.

"Message here from Kath, boss," Stella said. "Kylie has rented that flower shop for about five years. No problems until Covid. She made most of her money doing weddings, but that dried up. There were plenty of funerals, of course. But at the height of it all, flowers weren't allowed. She's deep in debt to suppliers, and overdrawn at the bank. Fell behind on her rent for a while but then she cleared the debt, but she never opened the shop again. The landlord talked to her about giving it up, but she didn't want to and he was getting his money, so he let things go."

It was about twenty minutes before the patrol car arrived. They sat in Jordan's car watching the pub and the car park and then, when the backup arrived with a flash of headlights, Campbell went back to the pool car with the comment that he hoped he hadn't just cocked up mightily.

They retraced the short route back to Allport Road.

Chapter 53

It was fully dark now. Not the best time to be scrabbling about in back alleys.

Campbell was finishing a call with his phone on hands-free as they parked up against the concrete block wall. "The post-mortem exam results have come through while I've been out," he said. "Notes from the medical examiner who has sent me a precis for now. Nothing that we weren't expecting. Just filthy murders of two inoffensive old people on their own, no family. That's not so unusual nowadays. But they had each other, and they were coping. It's so infuriating. After a decent, unassuming life, they end up dying like this."

Jordan nodded. It was that fury and sense of unfairness that could turn DS Campbell into a good copper. It was what drove him personally, and he had seen the same anger in Stella.

Underfoot was puddled and dirty, and Stella used the torch app on her phone to find the way. Jordan had a large Maglite in the car and when he came up behind her, she laughed and turned off the smaller beam. "Show off," she said. "Size isn't everything, you know."

There was no street lighting near enough to illuminate the narrow road, but there was a dull glow from a couple of the flats above the shops and the rear window of the off-licence. It was a short distance of just a few yards to the back gate. The old wood stuck and grated against the gritty floor and rattled as Jordan pushed against it. It wasn't locked, though, and with the combined efforts of Campbell and Stella, they were able to push it wide enough to slide through.

"Don't we need a warrant?" Campbell said.

"I thought I heard someone." Stella raised her eyebrows and grinned as she spoke. "Might have been a cat, but I think we should look."

Campbell lingered, taking the time to push the gate back into place before crossing the yard to catch up with them.

There were bars covering the windows, and the door was fastened with a hasp and staple and a hefty padlock. It would be a bridge too far to break in without the proper paperwork. Jordan bracketed his face with his hands and peered into the gloom. There were certainly no flowers inside. From the weak, reflected light leaking through from the main road, he could make out some items piled in a corner, and a table in the middle of the room. There was a chair lying on its side a few feet away. He puffed out a breath and shook his head. "Nothing to see."

Campbell's Airwave radio crackled into life. The patrol officers reported little activity in the time they had been there. One car had arrived, carrying what appeared to be two guests. The men had gone inside briefly, left their luggage and driven away. He spoke breathless with excitement. "They've left the pub, and it looks as though they're heading back this way. The patrol car is behind them. They want to know whether to stop them or simply follow."

"They could be coming back here. Tell the car to observe only and then if they turn into the access road to drive on. We should get back to the cars. Reverse to the garages, park outside the doors. With luck, they won't notice us."

Cold water splashed into Stella's shoes as she jogged back across the wet tarmac. "Sodding hell. Wet socks. I hate wet socks. How many times do we end up in bloody back alleys and rear entries?" she said as she threw herself onto the seat.

The white van pulled to a halt beside the gate and the driver's door was flung open. Kylie Heywood jumped down and marched towards the back gate. She didn't wait for the bald bloke from the other car, now parked behind, but got her shoulder to the wooden gate and forced it open.

The man followed behind, hunched, head down.

"What now?" Stella said.

"Just wait."

The interior light in Campbell's car flashed on as he opened the door. "Oh, shit." Jordan wagged a hand out of the window. "Shut your door, you pillock." He muttered.

Campbell didn't see or didn't understand the signal, and he slammed his door and ran forward. Stella leaned over and pushed open the rear door to allow him access. "What the hell?"

146

"What? Didn't you see they've gone inside?" he said.

"Of course we bloody saw, man," Jordan said. "Which is why we didn't open our doors and didn't turn the lights on. A hint for the future, mate. When you don't want to be seen, turn off your interior lights."

"Sorry about that. But they're inside."

"Were you not the one who was going on about a warrant not ten minutes ago?" Stella said.

"Well, yes. But they're here now."

"And?"

"We could go and knock, though, couldn't we?"

"And say what? 'Oh hello, can we just come in and look around?'" said Stella.

"Why not?"

Jordan interrupted the back and forth. "I reckon we're better just watching for now. This has not gone the way we thought it would. Better to see what they are up to, I reckon. Okay, Andy?"

"If you say so, sir. But I don't see…"

"If we go in there now, what have we got? What looks like an empty property, a possible police harassment claim from Kylie Heywood, and they'll know we're still watching them," said Jordan.

"Fair point. Okay. But if she gets away, I'll have to explain it to my boss."

"I've told you I'll take any flak. Right now, though, we have suspicion only. We need more or it'll be a replay of last time's no-comment interview."

They cut short any further discussion as Kylie Heywood emerged from the dark yard and opened the rear doors of the van. She dragged out a couple of large holdalls and carted them inside. Campbell wiped a hand over the steamy inside of the window and Jordan bit his tongue, thinking of how visible the smears were. He was still telling himself he liked Campbell, but irritation was nibbling at the edges.

After a while, there was the wavering beam of a torch flashing off the walls of the yard. Kylie and the bald man emerged and dragged the door closed. She turned and spoke. They couldn't make out the words, but the annoyance was obvious. She wagged her fingers in his face and then turned to the bigger vehicle, clambered in and slammed the door.

As she drove away, they expected the man to follow. "If you don't want to leave your car here, you best be ready to get out," Jordan told Campbell. "We might well be after them in a minute, and turn off the automatic interior lights."

The big, bald man peered back and forth along the alley and then turned round and leaned against the wobbly gate, pushing and shoving at it.

"Andy, get your arse in gear, mate. Follow Kylie, call in the patrol car to help you."

"What are you going to do?"

"Now, man. She's on her way. For Christ's sake."

Campbell opened the door. The lights were quickly extinguished. At least he was now sticking to the plan of not being seen.

As they watched the rear lights of the pool car disappear round the corner, Jordan and Stella left the Golf and crossed the alley to where Kylie's companion had now gone back into the rear entrance of the flower shop.

Chapter 54

Downstairs was unlit, but the door was unlocked, the padlock hanging loose in the staple. Stella and Jordan pressed against the damp wall. A dim light glowed from the upper windows. "The electric's on. That's interesting," Jordan said.

They crab-walked along the yard, pressing back against the dirty brick. Jordan reached out a hand and turned the old-fashioned knob. They heard the click of the lock. With just a glance at his sergeant, Jordan pulled open the door, and they stepped into the darkness.

There was the smell of damp and disuse. No scent of blooms or blossoms, and the table in the middle of the room was dusty and sticky.

The floorboard above creaked as the man moved across the space. They were at the bottom of the flight of narrow stairs now. There was the low rumble of voices.

Jordan reached out a hand to find the banister rail and, stepping on the edges to minimize any creaking, they climbed.

The top of the stairs opened to a narrow landing. Underfoot was dirty and the damp smell here was overlaid with a hint of uncleaned toilets. It wasn't pleasant.

A door opened onto one large room facing the front of the building, which was dimly lit by the streetlamps outside. It was empty. Broken blinds dangled from the window frames and in one corner was a heap of cardboard slowly sloughing away to become smelly garbage. They moved on to the next door, which was set at the rearmost side of the corridor. The door was ajar and Jordan held up his hand in warning. They listened to the conversation going on inside. One side of the debate was heated, a violent hissing of words answered by a dull monotone.

"She's gone, but she'll be back. You know that. What are we going to do, man?" said the angry voice.

"Just let me go. Don't be such a dick. What the hell is wrong with you, Brian? I thought we were mates."

Someone kicked out, probably at the wall, judging by the sound. "This is not the way it was supposed to be. Bloody hell," was the violent response.

"No, nobody was supposed to get hurt. That was never part of the deal." The speaker was overtaken by a bout of coughing. "Man, you just need to end this. We need to get away. Leave her to deal with the mess she's created, and we'll go. We can go away somewhere. I don't know, Europe, Thailand. Remember the times we had there? Come on. You're just making things worse. Unfasten these bloody ties and let me go. If you want to stay with her, okay. I don't know why you would, but if that's what you want, I'll go. I'll just go. You'll never see me again. How long have we been mates, eh? Brian? How long?"

There was a sigh. "I know, bloody hell, Tony, I know. But I'm so deep into this, now. She could finish it for me if she wanted to. She could really drop me in it. That bloke, the one off the bridge. That wasn't her, that was me — me and Doug."

"All the more reason why we should get the hell out of here. Doug's gone. He's got his head screwed on. He didn't hang around to get even deeper in the shit, did he? And what about her, those poor women? How can anyone do that?"

"Stop it." Brian's angry voice hitched up a notch. "Just stop it, yeah. I've told you. I can't leave her. I just can't."

"But she's evil, man. Really evil. Okay," Tony said. "Think about all the stuff we've been through together. Doesn't that mean anything now? The stuff we've had to do. The shit-hole places the Army sent us."

Stella had her phone out. She had leaned round to record the discussion. Jordan slid aside to give her space.

"I never wanted to get into this," he continued. "It's sordid. Taking advantage of helpless old people was bad enough, but this... now they're dead, man. Dead."

"It's not all her fault. She's as deep in crap as we are. It's not like getting an overdraft. These people she's dealing with are vicious. What do you think will happen to her now? She's not a bad person. She's just scared. She stuck by me, all this time, when I've been screaming at night, waking in cold sweats, having the flashbacks. She's been there for me. I tell you, she's not bad."

"Not a bad person. Oh, come on. She's filthy. Taking advantage of sad old men just so she can hold it over them. Poor old buggers. Probably been faithful all their lives until she came into it. Where is it going to end, eh? She's gone too far now. She could have carried on with her bloody flower arranging. Her weddings and funerals. What the hell. She'll never get out of it, and she's dragged us in it with her. I tried to help her. I did what you asked and took her to France and told her to stay there, told her to wait for you. She didn't, though, did she? No, she bloody didn't. She could have got away then, but she was so stupid."

"You just don't get it, do you? She couldn't pay the rent on this place. It's what happens. You have a dream, and it falls apart. You borrow a bit, you can't pay it back, you borrow a bit more, you can't go to the bank. You're trapped. Stuck. And then the sharks move in. All she wanted was to sell flowers. Things just got away from her. I tried to help, but you know I've got nothing. Yes, okay, we've been mates a long time but that was then, this is now, and this is what I have to do now."

"I could have got you work."

"Oh yeah, how could you have got me work? You're barely getting by. You're nearly as bad off as me, except you had your house, everything from when you were married. I never had that. No, I know we've been through it together in the past, but we're miles apart now and there's nothing you can do for me."

Now Jordan and Stella had enough. Although there were details still to fill in, they had the basics to arrest the two men. They didn't know if there were weapons. They knew that there had already been deadly violence. Jordan turned to look at Stella, her face lit by the glow from her phone. She clicked the off button, squared her shoulders, and nodded.

Chapter 55

Jordan never made any fuss about his circuit training or his work with weights. For him, it was just what he did when he could fit it in. His mum and Nana Gloria had encouraged fitness. His dad died young of a heart attack and his death had seen a sea change in the family outlook. Apart from anything else, his fitness training kept him away from the gangs and drugs that haunted the part of London he had grown up In. He was tall at over six feet. He was young, still in his thirties, and he was extremely athletic.

As she watched him flex his shoulders and take in a deep breath, Stella was more than happy to let him take the lead as they burst open the door to the dim upper room and he charged forward, yelling out. "Police. Down on the floor. Lie on the floor. Do it now."

The stunned moment of immobility was followed by noise, a flurry of action, yelling and the stomp of feet as the man from the pub tried to dodge past the bulk of Jordan, who was blocking the doorway. Stella had ducked inside and run to Tony Yates, who sat on the floor under the window, fastened to a radiator with white plastic ties around his wrists, and black heavy-duty ones around his ankles. There was a bottle of water beside him, although how he was supposed to have reached it was anyone's guess. He had been there long enough to stain his trousers with urine, and he turned away from her prying eyes in embarrassment.

"Get me loose, yeah?" he said. "I won't run, but my arms are agony. Just let me loose."

On the other side of the room, the two men were locked in an exchange of fists and feet. They were well matched, and neither looked to have the upper hand. Jordan bent slightly and charged like a bull at the bald bloke. The collision knocked the air from his lungs, but he had dodged sideways, and the full force of the impact was lost. Jordan was unbalanced and staggered a few more steps towards where Stella was crouched. She had cut through the cable ties with her penknife but snapped a handcuff on one wrist and used the other side to retether Tony to the radiator.

The other man didn't hang around. He used the momentary advantage to dart through the door and out onto the dark landing. Jordan was quickly after him, yelling at him to stop.

"You." Stella pointed at Tony Yates, who was easing his sore shoulders and shuffling his feet, which were still tied. She picked up the bottle of water and thrust it at him. "Don't you bloody move." She didn't wait for a response before she joined the chase.

Out on the landing, Jordan had reached the fleeing Brian and grabbed his shoulders, spinning him round and wrapping his arm around the man's neck. He had locked his hand around his wrist and dragged the bloke to the ground, kicking and squirming, his fingers tearing at Jordan's arm.

Stella kept clear of the thrashing feet but threw herself bodily onto Brian's back. It was enough, and Jordan could release the strangle hold before he caused anything more than panic and submission.

It was over, and they called for transport. One was definitely for a prisoner; although they knew Tony Yates was up to his eyes in what had been going on, they decided an ambulance for him would be best. They wouldn't risk future problems from clever lawyers who would complain about neglect or lack of care.

Jordan was trying to raise Andy Campbell, who was out on the road chasing the white van along with the patrol car. Stella didn't want to go in the ambulance, but someone had to. In the end, they sent a complaining and disgruntled patrolman who was not pleased at missing out on what looked like a more exciting option than sitting in a curtained cubicle in an A&E department. For his part, Tony Yates was happier to be under the care of paramedics than the police.

Chapter 56

Jordan left the scene to be secured by the patrol car driver. The two men were taken away, one to languish in the hospital and one to wait it out at Birkenhead Police Station.

They drove out onto the main road, Stella using her Airwaves set to raise Andy Campbell. "Do you have her?"

The lack of response told them as much as they needed to know. "Working on it. She gave us the slip. We lost her at Raby Mere."

"Jesus, how could you lose her at Raby Mere? There's nothing there."

"She abandoned the van, and she's off in the woods somewhere." They could hear him thrashing about breathless in the dark. "She's got to be here somewhere. I'll find her."

"Yeah, you probably won't, will you? It's all fields and woodland there. Are there even any streetlights? Secure the van and wait," Stella said.

She threw the handset onto the dashboard. "What a wally. What an absolute waste of skin. It was a van, for

Christ's sake. How hard can it be to catch a bloody white van?"

"Nothing much we can do now, in the dark. We'll alert the patrols in the area. Best hope is to get the chopper up. Let's get back to the station and see if they'll authorise it. If not, I'll get on to DCI Lewis and see if he can pull some strings. No point having people staggering about in the fields. If she's still there, the infrared camera will find her. If not, we're going to have to expand the search quickly. She's on her own now and probably panicked, so who knows which way she'll run? We need to find out more about her background. Get Kath onto that first thing."

"Maybe she'll go back to Aintree; back to Tony Yates's mother's house," Stella said.

"Hmm – would you?" Jordan said.

"I don't know, do I? I've never blackmailed old blokes and suffocated crippled pensioners, have I?"

Jordan didn't respond to the outburst.

"Sorry, sorry, boss."

"It's okay, it's frustrating, but we'll find her. We've got the other two, anyway."

"Yeah. I know. It's not that, though."

"Okay, what is it then?"

"Geoff."

"Your uncle?"

"Yep. That call I took. Apparently, nobody knows where he is. He was supposed to be going to the alehouse with my granda. He didn't turn up and when they went round to his flat, he wasn't there. No sign of him, and the place was dark and cold, but the door was unlocked."

"Shit, you should have said."

"We had enough on, and this was personal."

"Not really. If it looks as though he's in trouble, it's not personal anymore, is it?" Jordan turned to look at her and saw the shine of tears on her cheeks.

"It's my fault, isn't it? He said I should never have interfered. I don't know what I should do now," she said.

"You do know. You should treat this like a crime. Look, I'll go into the station at Birkenhead and interview Brian. I'll get things set up so that when Tony Yates is released from the hospital, he's brought back there. He's already under arrest. We've got the recording and our own witness statements. It's just going through the motions with them now. We'll leave Andy Campbell to organise the search for the woman. So, you head back now and start the ball rolling there. I'll join you as soon as I can."

They turned into the car park at Birkenhead. "Take my car back. I'll grab a lift as soon as I've finished here. If he's got any sense, he'll just tell us what the hell has been going on. If he goes down the solicitor and no-comment route, I'll leave him to stew overnight, okay?"

"Thanks, boss."

"Don't thank me. This is the job. Try to keep it at arm's length if you can. That probably seems impossible right now, but you'll do better."

"Bloody Geoff, I never really liked him."

Chapter 57

Jordan didn't give Brian Boland long to answer his questions. The man knew he was caught and surely understood he was only playing for time. He asked about Kylie and was told that they were looking for her. After that, he asked for a solicitor, and it was the end of the session.

Campbell trailed back into the station, his tail between his legs and mud on his clothes. "We're bringing the van back."

Jordan told him they were mobilising the helicopter from Hawarden. "If she's still there, they'll find her. What you need to do is get things set up, so that everyone is on the lookout for her if she still isn't found by first light. Get some troops to search all the usual places: barns, garages, sheds. Knock on doors. You need to prepare something for the press. Get onto that as soon as your press office is working. It is imperative that we find her. You really can't fart about with this. Have you spoken to your boss?"

"Tried to, but it went to voicemail. He'll be in tomorrow, probably around ten-ish. That's his usual time."

"In that case, you need to get a grip."

"We're short of bodies. They only gave me a small team. This was just a suspicious death. We weren't even sure there was anything dodgy at first and things have escalated. Then when you came over, DCI Harkness said I should just do as you said. I don't want to keep calling him. It'll make me look like a wally."

"But you have to move this along."

Campbell lowered his head for a minute and puffed out something between a groan and a sigh. "What about the two blokes?" he asked.

"One is in the detention suite waiting for a brief. Tony Yates is still up at Arrowe Park Hospital."

"Where's DS May?"

"On her way back to Liverpool, she has stuff going on there that needs her attention."

"So, what should I do now?"

Jordan stared at him for a moment, nonplussed. "I thought I'd made it clear. You deal with setting up the search for the girl and have SOCO go to the flower shop. I'm heading back to Copy Lane, but I'll call in at the hospital on the way and have a word with Tony Yates. Maybe if I catch him before he's brought here, he'll be more likely to talk."

"Shall I come with you?"

"No. Don't you think you've got enough to do here?"

Jordan wanted Tony Yates on his own, the way it had been at his house.

* * *

The hospital emergency department was night-time quiet, slightly less busy than during the day. There were patients waiting, as always, and a line of ambulances in the bay. Jordan showed his warrant card to the receptionist. The man grunted and waved a hand toward a nurse who was entering data into a computer. Jordan waited until she had finished and looked up to glance at his ID. "You've got Tony Yates here. He should have a police escort. I need to have a word."

She clicked and scrolled, nodded, and then held up a finger. "One sec."

It was more than a second, but eventually they showed him into the cubicle. Tony Yates was dressed in a hospital gown and sitting on the edge of the examination couch. His clothes were in an evidence bag on the floor.

The patrolman was dozing on a chair in the corner. He shook himself awake. "Boss. Waiting for a doctor to sign his discharge. He's okay, a bit dehydrated, bruises, a possible cracked rib, and wounds to his wrists and ankles."

"I am here, you know," Yates said.

Jordan nodded at the bobby. "Why don't you get yourself a coffee? You look as though you need it. Be about ten minutes, yeah," Jordan said.

They watched the officer leave, and Jordan pulled the chair away from the wall. He sat on the narrow plastic seat, rested his elbows on his knees, and lowered his face to his hands. He rubbed his eyes and came up blinking. It was going to be a while yet before any chance of a rest. He sighed.

"Look, I haven't got long, but I want to understand what's happening here. I have to tell you – we heard a lot of the conversation between you and Brian Boland. We have some of it recorded. You don't have to talk to me right now, but you might as well. You'll still have to make a statement, but Kylie's missing and anything you can tell me might help us find her. Now, from what we heard, you had nothing to do with the deaths?"

"No, well, yes. You're right. I didn't kill anyone. That wasn't me. I never saw any of it. I'm in deep shit, I know that, but I didn't do that."

"Okay, so what are you mixed up with here, Tony?"

Yates closed his eyes for a moment and then shrugged. "We were in the army together, me and Brian and another mate Dougie Waters. We were close. I don't know if you understand what that means?"

Jordan shook his head. "I never served, but it's easy to see it's a strong bond between people who did."

"Bloody right it is. Since we came back, he's sort of kept in touch, turning up now and again. He's a mess – PTSD, no job, no place of his own, and his family don't want to know him because he got into drugs a while back. If you come back with visible scars, you get sympathy – if you've got a limb missing, you have care. When it's invisible, it's different. Poor Brian, he's cleaned himself up a bit, credit where it's due, and that wasn't easy for him. He's off the drugs and he was trying to sort it, but it's so hard. He's broken, to be honest."

"And Kylie?"

"Bloody Kylie."

Tony lowered his gaze to the floor and spoke in a low monologue, stopping now and again to sip water from a plastic cup. He had tried to help his friend out several times and when he formed a relationship with Kylie Heywood, had hoped it would be the saving of him. He'd always thought she was flaky, though. She had her own business, flowers, selling them, taking orders for arrangements. But when everything went pear-shaped with Covid, she got into a mess. When Tony's mum died and her house was empty, he let Brian live in it for a while, doing him a favour. He moved her in. Tony didn't like it. "But what could I do?" he said. "He was my mate." He shook his head.

"But how does all this tie in with what's happened with these victims?" Jordan asked.

Tony lowered his gaze, his shoulders slumped. At first, he didn't seem to be making much sense. He complained about the cost of home care. There had been a huge bill to pay each month for his mum and in the end, he had cancelled the carers to look after her himself. He looked up and leaned forward to make his point. "It's bloody hard and depressing."

Jordan nodded his understanding, and Tony continued. He had mentioned it casually, but Kylie had come up with the idea that she could provide care. She told them she'd volunteered when she was at school. "I don't even know if that's true, but she's convincing, and I wanted it to work out for Brian," Tony said.

Kylie had said she could do it cheaper if the council wasn't involved. It was running costs for the big businesses that kept fees high. So, if it was just her and only a few at a time, cash in hand, she reckoned it would work. The flower shop was closed, she had time, and she had transport – the van – but better still, a little old car that she'd inherited from her dad. They all realised it wasn't strictly legal, but they never saw the harm. Tony, with his work doing gardening and bits of decorating, was in a good position to find clients. He had made the connections between her and a few people in need of help.

"Then I told her about that poor sodding Tracy opposite me." He wiped a hand across his eyes. "I thought it was a good idea. It was. Then the bloke in New Brighton made a pass at her. He was old, but it didn't stop him or her. She egged him on. When she'd got him hooked, well, I suppose the only word for it is blackmail. That was it."

Tony and Brian had asked her to stop, but by then, she saw it as a way to get out of debt. Her life was in turmoil. She had become mixed up with loan sharks. They had made threats, and she was scared. Bullying vulnerable people seemed like easy money.

Tony shrugged his shoulders. "If she'd just given that bloke what he wanted, she could have made a bit on the side. It wasn't enough, though. Okay, we know what that is, but she could have made something there. Money for sex, it's all over the place. But then she saw he would want to keep her quiet." He stopped and sat in silence for a minute. "Poor Tracy. I knew her, and Stanley. How can I ever forgive myself for that? I'll never forgive myself for any of this. I didn't do it, but I'm guilty, aren't I? I could have stopped it."

He swiped at his eyes with the back of his hand. He struggled to regain control and took a gulp of his drink. Then he turned to look directly at Jordan.

"Look, you can see what happened. It just snowballed, and it got completely out of control. It was inevitable it was all going to come unstuck. Then Stanley didn't want to pay anymore, and he threatened her with the police. That's when it went completely out of control. That's when they did what they did. It was never supposed to end up like that. Nobody was supposed to get hurt." He buried his head in his hands and sobbed.

"And the trip to France?" Jordan asked.

"I was still trying to help. Brian's passport was out of date. I took her over there, found her a place to stay and wait. It was a crappy little Airbnb, but she didn't stay. Then, that bloke in New Brighton had a crisis of conscience and told his wife about what he'd done. Possibly, wanted a clean break before the new year or maybe too much of the Christmas spirit, who can say? Anyway, she rang and threatened Kylie. By then, she was in so deep, she'd gone a bit mad, I reckon. She panicked easily and couldn't cope on her own. She came back. Brian couldn't leave with no passport. She needed to be with him, she said. Him and Dougie, both my best mates, blokes from the army. Comrades, you know, well, now they were in it up to their necks, so there was no way out for anyone. I'd kept in touch with my muckers, and we were supposed to stick together, had to, it was non-negotiable, or so I thought. What a bloody mess, what a balls-up."

"When you told me you saw Stanley's car leaving that night, that wasn't true either?"

"No, it was hers. I reckon she was taking Doug and Brian off to meet Stanley. Dougie told me he thought he was going to make a last payment, and they'd leave him alone. If I'd known then what she'd done, and what they were going to do, of course I would have acted differently. I keep thinking maybe I could have saved Tracy, could have got some help for her. Of course, just then I didn't know what was happening with Stanley. I honestly didn't. But then I got a call from Dougie. I don't know where he was right then. It was the middle of the night, he was hyper, telling me what they'd done, saying he was leaving, and I should do the same, and everything went to shit. I'm sorry."

Jordan asked why he had never reported what had happened. He knew it was wrong, and he hadn't broken the law until he helped to cover it up.

"I was going to. I felt bad that I'd lied to you, and all of it. Look where it got me. I threatened to blow it all wide open. I told Brian and Kylie they had to give themselves up. Well, you saw what they did. Called me round to the house, 'to talk'." He flipped fingers in the air. "We were always well matched, and he's still a big bloke. I tried to fight him off, but I guess I held back. Fighting a mate, it's wrong. She hit me with a bloody bottle. She's mad, totally mad. I actually thought she was going to get him to kill me, for Christ's sake. Anyway, I'm not going to give you guys a hard time. I'll hold my hands up to my part in it. Believe me when I say, all I did was give them some names."

Jordan pointed out that he had done more than that. He was an accessory and there were the lies he'd told to obstruct the enquiry at the very least. There would be charges to answer, but he was sorry for the guy.

He mulled over everything he'd heard. Much of it was simply Kylie taking what she saw at first as an easy way out. He accepted that it had spiralled out of control, but it still didn't add up. Blackmail and fraud were crimes, but on this scale, it was small stuff. Prostitution at this level would barely register. How had it led to murder?

Chapter 58

Jordan sent a message to Campbell outlining his conversation with Tony Yates. He told him that the man was ready and willing to make a full statement when they took him back to Birkenhead Police Station. At least that should be straightforward.

The driver of the car he'd commandeered to take him to Copy Lane was happy to drive without talking, and Jordan sat in the rear. He laid his head against the seat and closed his eyes. The gentle rocking lulled him and he drifted into a doze. He opened his eyes briefly when the drone of the tyres changed and noted the passing flash of the lights in the Mersey Tunnel. It was quiet, and the driver had turned down the radio. There wasn't time for a deep sleep, but it was something, and he was up and awake as they turned into the car park in Aintree.

"Get yourself something to eat. They do a good breakfast if it's not too late. I owe you. Tell them I'll sort it out." The idea of free food made the driver smile, and he went off humming to find the canteen. Jordan hoped it was still early enough for the coffee to be unstewed and the bacon baps to be hot.

Kath was already in the incident room and John came over with his hand outstretched. "Glad to see you back, John," Jordan said.

It was surprisingly quick to bring them up to date with what had happened. He asked Kath to check HOLMES and the PNC to make sure Campbell had sorted things at his end.

"It's up there, boss. Everyone should be aware."

"Excellent. I shouldn't feel the need to check up on him, but he's inexperienced, just feeling his way into his first major case, and doesn't seem to have the backup he should over there. Anyway, he's got this sorted, so it's fine." His phone rang, and he waved it in the air. "Ha, talk of the devil."

Jordan raised a thumb at the others listening in the room, but as the conversation continued, he lowered to a chair and shook his head. Kath glanced at John and pulled a 'what the hell' face.

They understood that the helicopter had been out over the land at Raby Mere and found nothing with the forward facing infra-red camera. They searched by eye when the sky began to lighten.

Jordan ended the call and slid his phone onto the desk.

They waited.

"Found her," he said.

They still waited because they could tell that wasn't all.

Campbell had reported that they were sending in a recovery team. There was nowhere for the chopper to land, and they could tell it was probably too late anyway. They hadn't had any way to get to her. There had been a discussion about contacting RAF Valley, but in the end, it was decided that was a waste of time. She was half in and half out of the water, head down.

Jordan looked at the others. "Of course, they're cut up about it, but realistic. There is a team heading for her on foot now. The chopper is still hovering but will need to head back to base soon because of fuel and what have you. All very dramatic, but it's not going to end well. When she ran away, it was into dark and difficult terrain. There are slippery banks, tree roots, many hazards. She probably had no idea where she was, and she was panicked." He shrugged. The body would be brought to Liverpool for a post-mortem exam and Jordan asked John to attend. Before that, he suggested John arrange a meet-up with Campbell to establish a working relationship. They were going to have to co-operate with the Wirral force now to put both cases before the CPS. They had all the information they needed to report what she did, and now she was out of it. There was still Brian Boland and some ends to tie up with Tony Yates, and there was still another missing bloke. It wasn't over yet.

"Are you coming, boss?" asked John.

"Not at the moment. I think Stella needs some help."

"Where is she? I haven't seen her since I came back."

"Looking into something else. I'm going to get myself something to eat and a coffee; then I'm going to join her. Can you guys make a start on the paperwork?"

There was no satisfaction in solving the case, none of the usual banter and high spirits. Kath fired up her computer and John walked down the corridor, with Jordan leaving him at the door to the car park.

Chapter 59

Penny left a voicemail asking what his plans were. She tried to be considerate and non-confrontational, but he could sense a hint of frustration. Her sister had suggested a dinner get-together for New Year's Eve. The murders of Tracy and Stanley Lipscowe were solved. There would be a lot of tidying up to do. It was routine, and with the death of Kylie Heywood and the confession of Tony Yates, it could only be a matter of time until Brian Boland held his hands up to his part in it all. Even if he continued to deny involvement, Jordan reckoned they had enough to convince the CPS that they would get a conviction. They still needed to find the missing Doug, but Jordan was hardly going to do that on his own. It was under control. There should be time now for the family.

Before then, there was Geoff and Stella. Surely this was going to be some sort of misunderstanding, easily sorted out. Perhaps they had panicked unnecessarily. Feelings were running high. The man might well have been in touch by now.

Jordan phoned Stella. She was at her mother's house, and he could hear her little nephew in the background. Someone had obviously bought him a noisy toy for Christmas. It sounded over and over with a high-pitched warble. Eventually Stella muffled the phone, but he heard her yell for quiet. The baby began to cry.

Jordan hadn't had a chance yet to play with Harry and the toys they had chosen so carefully for Father Christmas to bring. He wanted, more than anything, to go home and be a dad.

Stella told him she'd been to the flat in Kirkby, where her uncle lived. There was no sign of him. The family had called him constantly and even touched base with his divorced wife. She knew nothing and hadn't spoken to him for months.

"I'll meet you there. Have you done anything about starting an official investigation?" he asked Stella.

"Honest to God, boss, I've been chocka just trying to calm my lot down. They're all over the place with their stories. Granda says he spoke to Geoff on Tuesday. He's not budging on that. Mam says she tried to ring him Wednesday and had no answer. It was late, after we saw him. I haven't told them about that, by the way. Granda is dead worried, and I didn't think it'd help. We had to dose him up and get him to go lie down earlier. He wanted to go see for himself. Most of the time I'm just trying to keep the peace and, every time I mention making it official, there's another barny. Like our kid said, our Geoff wouldn't want the rozzers involved. They forget what I am. Times like this, I'm just 'our Stel'."

Jordan grinned in spite of himself. She couldn't see it, but right then she really was just 'their Stel'.

"You can't wait any longer. I think it'll be better if I do it. Don't even tell them. Get me a recent picture of Geoff for an appeal and we'll move things along. Do the family need a liaison officer, or are you okay to take that role?"

"No way, boss. I'll do for one of them if I have to stay here any longer. I think they can manage, though. Everyone's here, drowning in tea but holding each other together. What's the deal with our case? Our other case?"

"We still have to find the second bloke, Dougie Waters, the second man from the bridge, but I think Tony Yates might help a lot with that. We'll have to go back to Birkenhead. They are holding them both there for the time being."

Stella asked about Kylie. Jordan had forgotten that she had been completely off the grid. He told her the woman had been found dead. "I've had a message just now to say that they'll be doing a post-mortem examination tomorrow. Looks as though she slid down the bank, banged her head and drowned. With luck, we'll have located Geoff by then and we can get back over there."

"I'll meet you at his flat. I've texted you the address."

* * *

The route to Kirkby took Jordan along the M57. As he drove under the bridge at Spencer's Lane, he noticed that there was still a sign asking for any information about the incident in the week before Christmas. It was time to take that down, and he sent Kath a message to contact the motorway police. Once the holiday was properly over, they could be inundated with calls about something that no longer held any mystery. He glanced in the rear-view mirror and wondered at the fear Stanley Lipscowe must have felt as they launched him over the railings. He hoped he had been so far out of it he hadn't realised what was happening. All the poor bloke had done was find some comfort in his difficult life. Now Kylie was dead, Tony was in hospital, Brian was in custody, and Doug was still out there.

Chapter 60

When Jordan arrived at the flat Stella was standing beside her car sipping from a thermos mug. She offered it to Jordan who couldn't resist once he smelled the coffee. She put the empty cup on the passenger seat and they walked across the pavement. The flat was cold. Stella said Geoff didn't believe in leaving the heating on when he wasn't there. The kitchen was untidy, with a couple of bowls in the sink, a ring of dried soup around the edge of one and crusted Weetabix on the other. There were crumbs on the breadboard.

The living room was messy. Pyjamas in a bunch on the settee and a half empty coffee cup on the floor beside it. A glass had fallen from a shelf in the corner and lay smashed, in a sticky puddle on the parquet tiles.

There was a landline phone on the windowsill. Jordan checked the answering service. The one recording was the faint sound of breathing behind a background hum, and then a brief noise – maybe a laugh, maybe something else. The time stamp was late on Wednesday night. That was after Jordan and Stella had spoken to her uncle.

"Number withheld, get Kath to follow up with that. The provider should be able to help," Jordan said.

"She's on it, but like everywhere else, getting attention at this time of the year is hopeless. She'll keep on going, though. Kath's like a little terrier. Stupidly, I tried 1471, no surprise when it wasn't there. It was a forlorn hope, as they say. Trouble is, I've been here and looked at it all, but it doesn't seem as though I've done anything else. I don't know when the SOCO team might be able to get here. They're short-staffed. I don't think it's very high on their priority list."

"Did you talk to Vickie?"

"She's still on the Wirral."

"Is she? I expected her to be back by now. They've got their own people, and we already know all there is to know from there, I reckon. Having said that, we know your uncle's DNA and prints will be all over this place. Any new ones will only be helpful if they're already on file."

"Could be, though, knowing his background."

"Perhaps hold off on that a bit. It would mean taking prints from all of your family. I wouldn't think you'd want that."

"No, but then again, they know he's missing. I reckon they'd understand. Shall I go for it?"

"Up to you. Have you spoken to the neighbours?"

"The woman who lives next door was away until Thursday morning and the family downstairs are foreign – Eastern European, I think – and they couldn't understand me. With a bit of pantomime, I got them to acknowledge who I was talking about, but then it was all head shaking and smiling."

"It could be worth bringing in an interpreter. First, we need to have a serious word with Carl Reynolds."

"I've tried to call him a few times. He hasn't answered. I've left messages. If anything has happened to my uncle, he's got to be in the frame for it. If anything has happened to our Geoff, I'll do for him. I will, boss. I know I shouldn't say that, and I know you could argue that Geoff's only got himself to blame, but I'm not having it."

"Call the station and have them send a car round to his house. Bring him in for questioning. It'll make him more uncomfortable than us turning up for a casual chat."

Jordan pulled his phone from his pocket and held it out so that Stella could see John's name on the screen. She nodded.

Jordan ended the call with a short laugh. "John's not impressed with Campbell."

"No surprise there, then. What's going on?"

"They're on the way back with Kylie for the postmortem examination. Jasper is still not available. Still with his wife in Wales. I don't think it matters that much and they're bringing in Phyllis Grant. Haven't seen her for ages, she's been away somewhere helping with mass graves. Bloody awful job, I couldn't do that. She's good, and it should be pretty straightforward after what she's just been doing. I don't think we need to attend. We have enough to do here."

Chapter 61

They went back to Copy Lane. Stella rang her family and told them someone would come around and they all needed to give their fingerprints. She had decided that at least it would make them feel they were doing something and they were part of the search. They sent patrol officers to bring in Carl Reynolds. They did their best, but he just wasn't there and nobody knew where he might be. His house was locked and empty. When they peered through the letter box, they saw a small pile of mail behind the door. He lived in a quiet cul-de-sac in Netherton. Neighbours kept to themselves. The front garden of the house was paved over to make a space for his car, but the woman next door hadn't seen it for a few days.

"Not since Tuesday or Wednesday she says," Stella told Jordan. "We know he was around on Tuesday. But we

170

don't know if he ever went home after we spoke to him on Wednesday. What a pain in the arse this is all turning into. I was hoping to go out with Keith from upstairs and his mates for New Year. They're all a bit mad and they have a good night. Most of them are gay and I like that nobody tries anything on. You can just relax and enjoy it."

"It might still be okay. I know you're thinking the worst. I don't blame you, but don't let your imagination run away with you."

Stella nodded and tried to smile. She tipped coffee into the filter and took the carafe out into the corridor to fill it from the water dispenser.

Jordan's phone rang. It was John on his mobile. "Okay, boss. I'm in Liverpool at the mortuary. Dr Grant has just finished the exam on Kylie. I reckon it might be best if you have a word yourself. She's here now."

"Hello, Phyllis, how are you?" Jordan said. "Glad you're safely back from foreign parts. We must get together soon. What's going on with our drowned lady?"

"She's not."

"Sorry?"

"I know you won't want to hear what I'm about to say, Jordan, but Kylie Heywood didn't die from drowning."

"But she was in the water. They said half in, head down." As he spoke, Jordan knew he was wasting his breath. If Phyllis Grant said that the woman didn't drown, then she didn't drown. So much for his reassuring speech of minutes ago. He looked at Stella and watched in sympathy as she flopped onto the edge of her uncle's couch. "I'll come down and have a word," he told the medical examiner.

"Oh, what now?" Stella said.

"Can open. Worms everywhere," he said.

She grinned at him in spite of herself.

"Okay, this is what we're going to do. I'm going down to the mortuary, up to you if you want to come with me. Nothing more to do about your uncle right now. We should make sure they mention him at roll call and have everyone looking for both him and Carl Reynolds. Ask one of the civilians to print out images, quick as they can, and have them distributed. I don't think we have enough yet to put out anything on the general media, but the lads on patrol will watch for them."

"Agreed. I'll come with you to town. Let me put the coffee in a go-cup. It might help to keep you awake. I reckon you need to go home and have a sleep. You look knackered."

"I am, but let's see what the situation is first, and then we regroup. I need to call Penny. She's not going to be happy."

"The woman's a saint. I'd have shown you the door years ago."

"Ah yes, but you haven't tasted my steak and kidney pie. That's enough to keep any woman with me."

"Yeah, right. You'll have to show me."

"And I will, when all this crap is sorted. Come on, you can drive. I reckon I'd be a hazard. I'm seeing double."

Chapter 62

It had been more than a year since Jordan had seen Phyllis Grant. She looked up from her desk as he entered the office. She'd put her thick auburn hair into a neat bun. Tiny lines at the corners of her brown eyes were perhaps new, but they sparkled as she came to hug him. She was wearing a navy dress and, from the way it hung on her body, it was obvious she had lost some weight, but he thought she was still gorgeous.

"Sorry about this. I bet you've cursed me all the way here," she said.

"Not at all. I have to admit it's a surprise. I thought the investigation was pretty much cut and dried. Sorry, I don't think you two have met." He introduced Stella. "This case has been a mess from the start. I only got into it because I couldn't mind my own business. I'll know better next time."

"You don't mean that." She offered them good coffee, which they refused, holding up their own half-full cups, but the chocolate biscuits were irresistible. Once they had settled, she pushed a file folder across the desktop. They read in silence for a while, Stella leaning over Jordan's shoulder and chewing into his ear until he glared at her and she backed off.

"So," Jordan said, closing the file. "She didn't drown; she was dead when she entered the water."

"Yes, for certain. Her death was caused by a blow to her head with a blunt instrument. There were tiny bits of wood in the wound and moss in her hair. It wouldn't have been immediately obvious to the first responders because the water had washed away much of it and her hair was thick enough to hide the damage, especially while it was wet and tangled. If I'd been there..." She stopped and shrugged. "But then, I wasn't, was I?"

"Moss," Stella said.

"Yes, I have sent samples off for analysis, but my opinion is that you'll find it all around those woods and on the murder weapon. That will most likely be a large tree limb. Good luck finding that in woodland. Of course, if your killer panicked and simply dropped it, then it might still be local to the discovery site. Your SOCO team will find it and it will be bloodstained."

"Shit, sorry, sorry, Doc. Excuse me just for a minute." He didn't call Campbell, though that would have been the correct procedure. "John, have they secured the site at Raby Mere?"

"They should have done. Hang on, I'll ask."

Jordan looked down at his hand resting on his knee and saw that he had instinctively crossed his fingers. Well, that wasn't going to help. He straightened them. In the background he could hear the conversation, but not clearly enough to pass on what was being said to the two women watching him.

When John raised his voice in a hurried back and forth, he knew. "Boss, Andy is here with me. They recovered the body, had a look around for her belongings, and then pulled out. The first responder pronounced death. There wasn't any doubt. She was head down in the water, unresponsive and with no pulse. Apparently, they spent more time with the van, even though that had already been gone over with a fine-toothed comb. They took her out of the water and sent for the coroner's transport. She was brought straight here. Are you at the mortuary now?"

"Yes. Where are you?"

"I'm in a caff down the road with Campbell. We'll come back there."

"No. Get back to Birkenhead. Call them. The woods at Raby Mere are a crime scene. Someone killed Kylie Heywood. Get on it, John, quick as you can. The murder weapon is probably a big tree branch, but definitely wood of some sort. Quickly, man. I'll be with you shortly. Campbell needs to inform his DI and set things in motion. This has all become very much messier, if that's possible."

As they drove from the mortuary past Lime Street Station and on towards the Queensway Tunnel, Jordan called DCI Lewis in Copy Lane to bring him up to date. The phone was on speaker and he had to lay a hand on Stella's knee to stop her from responding as she heard their boss ranting about loss of control and poor handling of the situation.

"You were supposed to be over there helping, DI Carr. I told George Harkness that he could leave it all in your hands. Now I find there's a murder scene that hasn't been secured and a suspect still in the wind. It appears you came back far too soon. This is out of control. We began with a bloke on a bridge, and we've ended up here with a total debacle. You need to get a grip, Detective Inspector."

There was no point arguing. It didn't feel right to drop Campbell in the shit. He would need to make a full report in due course, anyway. The DCI's familiar reference to George told them enough about the relationship between the two senior officers to make it clear that they should keep their opinions to themselves. "I'm on my way back there now, sir."

"Keep me apprised and don't drop the ball again, Jordan." With that, the call ended.

Stella took a breath, ready to rant, and Jordan turned to look at her and shook his head. "He has a point. I thought Campbell had it sorted, but I should have realised there was the chance that she didn't just fall into the water. He's out of his depth, excuse the pun."

"How the hell could you possibly know that this is how it would turn out?" Stella said.

"I couldn't. But the point is, I should have at least considered the possibility."

"God, you are so bloody reasonable, it's not on. Campbell's a total div."

"He's only just come into Serious Crime."

"I know, but he's trained. It's not as if he's just joined the job. He must have been around for a while and served probation, same as all of us. Did he not learn anything? Has he been walking around with his head up his arse for years?"

"Listen, we just need to deal with it now. Later will be time for recriminations and probably enquiries. I'm sorry. You'd rather be looking for Geoff."

"But we've done what we can for now. Geoff's more than likely going to turn up with a massive hangover and a sheepish look on his face. He comes a poor second to these dead pensioners, and now this girl. Okay, she might have been an evil bitch, but even an evil bitch doesn't deserve to be whacked with a tree branch and left for dead." She paused. "Well, maybe sometimes, eh?"

Chapter 63

The woods were a scene of intense activity. It was all a bit late, but for now, they would make the best of things. They had already lost most of the daylight and couldn't put floodlights across the whole area. There was police tape and a slew of cars, a crime scene van, and he saw the welcome figure of Vickie Frost rustling towards him in her scene suit with her plastic shoe covers in her hand. She waved.

"I wondered where you'd got to," Jordan said.

"I had some days off owing and thought I'd stay over here on the Wirral with a mate. We intended to see in the New Year together; she bought tickets and all of that, but now look, I've been roped in to help out here. I can't decide whether it was the wrong place at the wrong time or the opposite. I haven't had a proper look yet, and it's soon going to be too dark, but we'll make a start at least. Bit of a cock-up this, eh?"

"You could say that. On the upside, at least we know the who and the where, and we possibly know the why. We even have a fairly accurate when."

"Piece of cake, then – it's a doddle."

"Oh yes, all be done by bedtime."

"Speaking of which, you look a wreck. Although, I do rather like the unshaven look. Very butch. Not that you're ever anything other." She stopped, screwed up her face. "Okay, all getting a bit weird. Please ignore the last two minutes of conversation. You look tired, though, mate."

He was saved a response by the arrival of John and Campbell. He expected the junior officer to be subdued, but he just seemed excited. "Blimey, another one. Who would have thought? It's like that *Midsomer Murders* thing. Hard to know who's going to be next."

Jordan and John shared a look. "So, what exactly is the state of play?" Jordan asked.

"SOCO are going in now, boss. We're organising a fingertip search of the surrounding ground and tomorrow they'll bring in a diving team for the stream. No point now, it's too dark already." John said.

"Good enough. Andy, is your boss fully up to date?"

"Yes. He wasn't too happy, especially as he was planning a trip to Scotland over the New Year's weekend, but he's coming into the station tomorrow for a session. I just hope I'll have more to tell him by then."

"I wouldn't get your hopes up. Unless we're really lucky, it'll take ages to find the weapon – a piece of wood in a forest. Not the best, is it? However, we need to go over what we have. Stella has gone on to your station. She's putting together some ideas and setting up extra facilities in the room. We'll use the same one as before, obviously, because there is no doubt this is all part of the same case."

"Do you reckon it could be a relative of the oldies? You know, a revenge killing?" Andy said.

"As they had no relatives, it's unlikely and if it was someone connected with them, that would assume someone had blabbed about what was going on. Why would anyone do that?" Jordan said.

"Okay, yeah, that's right."

"However, there are another couple of hypotheses. We need to have Tony Yates brought back to the station for questioning."

"But he was already under arrest. He couldn't have been here," Campbell said.

"No, of course not, but he has information that we need, and we need it now. Just get that sorted, will you? We'll leave the experts to get on with things here. I'll have a word with the crime scene manager, make sure he's got my contact details and then we'll head back to Birkenhead."

Stella had the room ready and coffee in a thermos brought from the canteen. There were already pictures of the area of woodland, the body of Kylie Heywood, and close-up shots of the wounds to her head.

John took a chair close to the front, with Campbell beside him. There were a few uniformed officers who had worked beyond the end of shift and stayed on, partly for the brownie points and, with at least some of them, because they were interested in solving the murder.

It was late. Jordan was exhausted and didn't want to mess about going over things that they already knew or that were in the HOLMES records, the PNC and on the other whiteboard.

"As far as I see it," he began, "there are two possibilities. We know the victim had pissed off some nasty people, moneylenders and the like, and been threatened by them. We will need to find out more about them. Fortunately, we have Tony Yates and now that he's admitted to his part in this mess, he has nothing to lose, so I feel sure he'll give us some information. What he has might be limited. I need from you, DS Campbell, information on likely subjects. They could be based in Liverpool, and I have already spoken to two of my best officers to send lists with current whereabouts of moneylenders, your known drug dealers and the like, with a history of violence. You must have names of people in your area so, quick as you can. We need to get on the streets tomorrow and do some interviews." He turned to scan the board.

"The second option is the missing member of this little cohort. At the moment, what we know is that he was a big bloke, probably shaven headed and has been seen wearing a long leather coat. That isn't much, I know, but once we have a chat with Yates, we will have more."

"I thought they were mates," Campbell said.

"Yep. That's what we were told, but now that everything has gone pear-shaped, it has more than likely screwed that up. How much remains to be seen. Tony Yates was their mate until they tied him to a radiator and beat him up. I can't believe that enhanced the friendship. Once we have a clearer description, as many people as possible need to be scanning CCTV. The shops, the pub, and Raby Mere. Hopefully, the SOCO team will bring us something, but it's raining. It's the worst sort of location and we really need to move on the assumption that what they find will be the devil's own luck. I say this with the greatest respect for Vickie and her team. If it's possible to find something, they're the people to do it, but we need to get moving ASAP. Everybody happy with that?"

There was a mumble of acceptance around the room. The door swung open and the sergeant from reception waved a hand at Jordan. "Your prisoner has arrived, sir."

Chapter 64

Tony Yates was red-eyed and unshaven. They had given him a plastic beaker of water and he wrapped his hands around it but made no effort to drink. As Jordan and Stella entered, he turned to look at them. He didn't speak.

They activated the recording equipment and went through the identification routine. Jordan nodded to the officer at the door who left, pulling it closed quietly behind him. "How are you, Tony?" Jordan asked. There was a shrug in response. "Do you need anything?"

Tony lowered his head and shook it slowly from side to side. "Only thing I want is to go back to how things were. I was doing okay, you know." He glanced up briefly. "It wasn't anything special, my life. I had my mam round the corner, jobs I enjoyed doing and my army pension for security. Now, there's nothing. My mate's a murderer. Those poor people are dead, and even bloody Kylie. Stupid bitch. Why did she run? She should have known she couldn't get away. They didn't tell me what happened, just that she was dead in the water. She could swim, I know that. So what happened?"

"That's what we're trying to find out," Jordan said. He asked about the loan sharks. For a moment there was a flash of passion in the other man's eyes, and he told them he'd help them as much as he could if it meant they might be caught.

Jordan had gone over and over what he had already been told, and there were things that still didn't add up. This was the chance to have it all make more sense. When he asked why Kylie still kept the shop, still paying rent she couldn't afford, Tony said that he had asked her the same thing himself.

He had told her she should give up on her dream. It was already too late. The sharks wouldn't let her. They paid the rent and added it to her debt. She wasn't allowed to re-open. "That would have made her happy, I think. That was all she wanted at first."

Jordan waited; Tony filled the silence. Kylie had been told to keep away from the place except for when they had her pick up bags from a house in Bromborough or brought to various locations. She took the bags to the shop in the van, left them in the rooms upstairs and went away again. They told her never to look in the bags and warned her she was being watched. "She didn't trust anyone, not even Brian. She was a wreck. I truly think she'd lost her mind in the end. Surely, she must have, otherwise she couldn't have done what she did."

He didn't think she was scared of being accused of prostitution by an old man, nor of blackmail by anyone. She wasn't bothered about operating as a carer without a licence. None of that troubled her. What she was scared of was being seen talking to the police.

Tony looked up now and leaned across the table towards them. "She didn't know who could be watching her or when. Every day she was looking over her shoulder," he said. "I reckon that she truly believed that being arrested would get her killed. She never said who they were, but she was terrified of them. I know that. She was a wreck. You should ask Brian. They were close. When she went off to look after the oldies, he went along in the van, waited until she was home safe. It was pathetic, really. She was terrified of being on her own. She might have told him who they were. Might not have done, mind you."

Jordan told him they wanted to give him the chance to talk to them first. "Anything you have for us could benefit us both. You help us now, Tony, and I'll make sure the right people know about it. It could be a factor when it comes to sentencing."

Tony turned his head to stare directly at Jordan. "Do you think I give a shit about sentencing? It doesn't matter what happens to me now. Those people are dead, and I could have stopped it. I went along with it, even though I knew it was wrong and it could all go tits up. They can lock me away for good. I don't care."

Stella leaned forward. "I know it all looks very black right now, but there is some future for you, Tony. You haven't killed anyone," she said. "Let's talk about your other mate. Do you really not know where Dougie Waters has gone?"

"Dougie. No, I haven't a clue. He buggered off pretty sharpish when things got sticky."

"How involved was he with the blackmail and the killing?"

Tony closed his eyes and drew in a deep breath. "You're asking me to drop my mate in it."

He obviously didn't realise how damning the statement was. Stella nodded. "We have a good idea about his part in all of this, but why don't you tell us from your side?"

Tony spoke in a low monotone as he told them that Dougie was often merely hanging around. They had done some moving, bits of furniture, stuff to the tip, clearing out sheds. It had all been odd jobs. Tony liked it because he could work when he wanted to, and it was mindless, just physical work. They had drunk together, played video games and just been mates. "That's all," he said. "We were just mates, the three of us, until Kylie came along to screw things up. I didn't know he'd had anything to do with that poor bloke across from me. Not until afterwards. He rang me in a proper mess. He asked for money to get away. I agreed to get Kylie off to France. I should have told them all to eff off right then, but mates are mates, aren't they?"

"Did you give him money?" Jordan asked.

"I didn't have any to give him. So, no. I used my credit card for air tickets and stuff for France, but he wanted cash. I didn't have no cash."

"Could Kylie not give you any money?"

"Kylie?" Tony made a noise, something between a laugh and a groan. "Kylie didn't have nothing. She was so deep in hock that any money went straight to those blokes. She thought she could get out from under. Doing their deliveries and paying them back, but the debt just kept getting bigger and bigger with the interest and the shop rent. I don't think you have any idea how bad all this was. It was sordid and scary and filthy." It was all too much. Tony lowered his head and covered his face with his hands. The plastic beaker tipped, spilling water across the table to drip onto his lap, but he didn't react.

"We're going to give you a break, Tony," Jordan said. "We'll take this up again later. Try to relax, yeah."

On the way out, Jordan stopped to have a word with the custody sergeant. They needed to put the prisoner on suicide watch and take him back to the custody suite.

"Does he need a doctor?" the sergeant asked.

"I suppose we'd better. Probably means we won't be able to question him any more right now. Let's just call it a night."

"Did you get what you wanted from him?"

"Not really. We'll interview Brian Boland, but might as well wait until tomorrow now. It's too late to bring him in, eyebrows would be raised because of the time."

They turned to leave.

"Detective Inspector," said the sergeant.

Jordan looked back. "Yeah?"

"Happy New Year. When it gets here."

Chapter 65

Jordan looked at his watch as they walked to the car. He showed her the time. "It's actually New Year's Eve already, Stel. Just a few hours before the fireworks and what have you. Time to go home."

He could tell by her face that the idea didn't fill her with excitement.

"Geoff?" he said.

"I've tried his phone again, no answer. Granda'll be upset, and that means me Mam will be edgy and narky. They don't want to know about my job most of the time, but right now they expect me to sort this out. They've had their fingerprints taken and my brother Pete's getting in a strop about that now. He wants me to fix it, but not if he has to do anything. Don't get me wrong, I don't think Pete's been up to anything dodgy, but you know what people are like. They're all 'my human rights' and 'nanny state' and what have you, and he's a bit of a div, just between you and me. So, he's winding them up. Vickie asked me if I wanted to go out with her mates. I think I might do that. There's nothing more I can do about Geoff. Just wait and keep on trying to reach him."

Jordan reiterated they could do more than that. The conversation in the Black Bull pub with Carl Reynolds made it clear that there was a definite threat, and with no sign of her uncle for days now they had good reason to put something on HOLMES, start enquiries and have notifications posted on the various force websites and Facebook pages. He knew the action would upset Stella's grandfather, but doing nothing was no longer an option. He put all this to her, and she agreed. "Let's leave it till tomorrow. I'm still hoping that maybe he's out on the lash and he'll turn up. I've tried that bloody Carl's phone, but I don't think it's turned on. There's not even a message."

They both knew how suspicious that was, and her eyes flooded with tears. He knew she was trying not to overreact, but was very worried.

Jordan nodded. "Go back to Liverpool. We'll get things moving. I know it's the worst possible day to start something like this, but we'll do it, anyway. In the meantime, try and get some rest. John's heading back. You can cadge a lift with him. Then why not come back and go out with Vickie and her mate, or just do what you originally planned and go out with your friend from upstairs? You can either have a rotten evening with your family and then Geoff turns up, or you can have a decent night and Geoff turns up."

"Or he doesn't."

"But whatever you decide won't influence that at this stage, will it?"

"No, I guess not. What are you doing?"

"I'm going back as well. But I have a couple of other things I need to do first. I'll see you at the station tomorrow lunchtime. We'll go for a drink, if you like, once we've got things on the go with the hunt for Geoff. Try to get in the mood."

Campbell had strolled out into the car park on his way home. He wasn't happy with the plan to meet again on the Sunday, New Year's Day, to continue the interviews, but knew better than to argue. Nobody wanted to transport prisoners and set up interview rooms on New Year's Eve and Jordan acknowledged that swimming against the tide wasn't going to win them any favours.

Chapter 66

The circus in the woods had been reduced to one patrol car in the road, and tape tied between trees and bushes beside the little river. Jordan pulled on his wellies and took his big Maglite out but it wasn't long until he realised that there was nothing for him to see. Sometimes re-visiting the crime scene was a help, but the dark water of the mere rippling quietly against the shore and the rustling, creaking branches moving in the wind weren't telling him anything except that he was alone. Footprints, broken twigs, scuffed ground, it would all be in the report from the crime scene manager and the SOCO team. He wasn't going to unearth some hidden clue like a detective on the television, and he soon knew that.

It wouldn't take long to drive back through the empty streets to Allport Road. It was on the way home. Just a quick visit to refresh his mind with the layout and atmosphere of the place where he'd fought with Brian and rescued Tony. Visiting now, with the extra knowledge and less of the tension, would freshen his memory; keeping it all fresh in his mind would help with the next interview.

He pulled onto the empty concrete slab at the end of the row of garages, turned the heater to high and rooted in the glove compartment for the chocolate he knew was there and his copy of the key to the shop. He sent a text to Penny to let her know he'd be back and was looking forward to having breakfast with her and Harry. For just a moment, he lay his head against the rest. It would be so easy to sleep. He should give it up now and have a break. Just one more thing so that he had everything clear in his mind, and then he could leave it until after the weekend.

The entrance to the backyard of the flower shop was still taped, but there was no bobby on duty. He lifted the plastic strip to duck underneath. There had been more tape across the shop door fixed to the frame. It had loosened and flapped against the wall. The doorknob turned easily in his hand, and the old wood swung open silently. There could be no technicians here now. He would have seen their van outside, and at this time in the early hours of the morning, the idea was ludicrous. They wouldn't have left the door unlocked. If they had, then there would be hell to pay the next time he spoke to them. He didn't believe that had happened.

He slid into the downstairs room. Flashing his torch beam across the table and shelves, he saw the marks of fingerprint powder. There were still a couple of evidence tents on the floor. So, the job wasn't quite finished. Still, they wouldn't have left without securing the premises. It was basic routine.

The creak of floorboards above his head made the hairs on his arms prickle and although he had been half expecting it, his heart gave a jump. He turned off the torch. There was enough light leaking through the dirty windows from the road outside.

He could call out. If he did that, there would be a couple of possible results. A voice from upstairs would identify themselves and all would be well. There could be nothing, just silence waiting to be investigated. There could be a response, a name, a question thrown back at him. It could be Campbell, stewing over the cock-ups and hoping for something to surprise them with. Of the three, silence was probably the most likely. Then there was the other possibility, the thunder of feet on the stairs and ensuing mayhem.

He weighed up the options, and he didn't call out. He moved quietly to the bottom step and listened in the darkness.

Chapter 67

The noises from the rooms above could only be made by a person. It wasn't an animal. Animals don't close doors, and they don't flush toilets.

Jordan hefted the big torch in his right hand and trod quietly up the scruffy staircase.

It would have been wiser to go to his car and wait for backup. Now it was too late. He was committed. To go out would mean turning his back on the landing, and that wasn't going to happen. He saw no option but to finish what he'd started.

If this was the thugs that Kylie had been involved with, he could be in deep trouble. If it was them, then they had to be stopped. He wasn't stupid and knew that this could end badly. He needed backup.

He could send a text to Stella. She would still be on her way back to Liverpool with John. They could be with him quickly, or better still they could raise the alarm with the local force. There would be a problem if they were in the old tunnel, then it was a lost cause because there was no phone signal. By the time they reached the exit and saw his message whatever was going to happen here would be all over. It was still the quickest option. She was number two on his speed dial, just two clicks of the buttons.

But he had sent the message to Penny and slid the phone onto the dashboard while he ate his chocolate. Stupid error. He knew it was irresponsible to carry on working when your brain was addled with exhaustion, and this was the result.

Okay, he had no phone. He had his torch, and he had the element of surprise, but it was so much more sensible to go back to the car. He began to turn on the narrow step.

The attack, when it came, flew out of the darkness with the scream of a banshee. One minute he was standing at the top of the staircase and the next a dark figure hurtled across the landing, fists flying, the whole weight of a body behind it. He raised his arms, but the impetus was too strong. They bumped against the banister and fell, locked together onto the stairs. Neglected old wood balusters cracked and broke and they fell through, two and a half meters to the floor below. The old table broke their fall, collapsing under the weight.

There was no time to assess damage. Jordan rolled and scrabbled to his knees. The torch had flown from his hand in the attack and slid into the corner, still lit. The beam shone across the grubby floor, illuminating a couple of upturned evidence tents. Vickie was going to be bloody angry he'd disturbed her crime scene.

The noise behind focused his mind on the current situation, and he spun to see the hulk of a man who could surely only be Dougie Waters struggling to his feet. His long coat was wrapped around his legs, and he fought to free himself from the flaps of leather.

Jordan knew even as he did it that it was ludicrous, but he began to recite, "Dougie Waters, I am arresting you on suspicion..." Dougie ignored him.

They were well matched. Jordan was over six feet and strong, but so was the other, and he really didn't want to be arrested. He stepped forward, arms raised, legs slightly bent at the knees. It was obvious he knew what he was doing.

Jordan glanced around in the gloom. He didn't want to fight with Dougie. If it came to it, he thought he'd make a good showing, but physical harm to a prisoner would never go down well, especially when there were no witnesses. He tried again to calm the situation. "We don't need to do this, Dougie. Why don't you just tell me your side of the story? We can sort this out. Enough people have come to harm. I think you were just trying to help Kylie."

In response, Dougie moved forward another couple of paces. He swore and gave what could only be described as a snarl. "Don't give me that. I'm not stupid," he said. "There's nothing down for me if I let you take me in. How about you turn away? Who's to know? Just keep your trap shut and I'll vanish. You don't want to take me on. I know you don't. This could be over right now, no problem. Kylie, bloody woman. I knew she was trouble from the start, anyway, she got her comeuppance, didn't she? People get what they deserve in the end. She screwed us all up, and she'd have dropped me right in it. Look at it this way: I was saving the country money. Now you don't have to put her in jail. But you're not taking me in, not for her, and not for that randy bugger in Aintree."

When he was in uniform, Jordan had used his ASP twice. He'd never had the need to actually strike anyone with the extending baton. Drawing it and flicking it open with the vicious hiss and click of noise had been enough to subdue the thug who had squared up against him.

But detectives don't carry ASPs.

There was no chance he was going to talk himself out of this, so Jordan braced his shoulders and lowered his chin, ready to take the attack.

As Dougie rushed forward, Jordan ducked away towards the middle of the room. The other man turned quickly. He was light on his feet for a big man, and well trained by the army.

Jordan held up his hand. "Stop, Dougie, really just stop."

Dougie didn't stop.

He charged again.

Jordan dived to grab at his legs and take him off balance. Dougie stumbled, but he didn't fall, and was ready to come again. Jordan scrabbled among the broken parts of the table in the middle of the room. He grabbed one of the legs that had broken loose. It wasn't particularly heavy, but it was a weapon of sorts, and he pushed to his feet, hefting it across the front of his body.

Dougie smiled and shook his head. There was to be no easy way out of the situation, but he was going to go down fighting. He had nothing to lose.

With a yell, he launched himself across the room, storming through the pile of broken wood. Jordan raised the table leg and readied himself to deliver the blow.

A figure flying in from the side, partly illuminated by the beam of a torch, confused and befuddled him. Then there was Stella yelling at the top of her voice for Dougie Waters to stand down and back off. John had Dougie on the floor, rolling and scrabbling in the broken wood and dirt, and Jordan threw himself into the attack. Between them, they had him subdued and handcuffed before Stella could finish her call for backup and the request for prisoner transport. She flicked the light switch and strolled over to where the three men were still pushing and shoving at each other.

"I reckon that's enough, lads. Jordan, your wife needs a call. She's in a bit of a state and you" – she pointed at Dougie – "stop being such a dick. Don't you know when you're beaten?" Then she recited the arrest for suspicion of the murder of Stanley Lipscowe and had him acknowledge he understood his rights.

Chapter 68

They didn't wait long for the blare of sirens to cut through the early hours. By the time Dougie Waters, hands handcuffed behind him, was escorted from the back door of the flower shop, lights were lit in most of the flats above the other retail units. A couple of hardier souls, wrapped in blankets or waterproofs, had come out onto the walkway to watch the show. It was brief and unsatisfying for the spectators, but Jordan gave Stella a quick hug before they left to join the patrol officers. "Bloody hell, was I glad to see you, mate."

"Penny is the one you should thank. She was sitting up fretting when she got your message. She tried to call you back, and she didn't mess about when there was no answer. She used the tracking app you've got on your phone and saw that your car wasn't moving. Google Earth showed her the dodgy location and she called me. Good job. A couple of minutes later and we'd have gone into the tunnel. Still, knowing Penny, she'd have sorted something. You've probably got a couple of missed calls from her. You need to let her know you're okay. Maybe don't tell her you've ripped your trousers, though. Leave that as a surprise, yeah?"

As the prisoner transport left the back road – no sirens, no need – Campbell drove up to park beside Jordan's car.

"Is it true you've got Dougie Waters, and he's coughed for Kylie Heywood?"

"You just missed him," Jordan said. "They're taking him to the custody suite so they can have him checked over by the nurse. I reckon he's okay, but best to be sure. I'm going home now. You can start the questioning about

Kylie if you like. He pretty much already admitted it to me, but you need to make it official. I don't reckon you'll have any trouble hanging on to him until Monday; we'll come back then to have a word about Stanley Lipscowe and dot all the 'i's on that one."

"Excellent, this is going to look great on my clear-up rate. Hey, I owe you one, mate." Campbell held out his hand.

Jordan shook it briefly. "Yes, you do."

The DS turned to grin at the others in the group. Stella shook her head and turned away with an audible tut.

As she opened the car door, she called over to where Jordan was dialling Penny's number on his mobile. "See you for brunch at the Premier Inn. Get yourself some kip first," she said.

Jordan raised a thumb and slid into the driving seat as his wife answered the call.

* * *

Penny let him sleep until almost eleven and the five hours were enough. She brought him a huge cup of coffee and an excited toddler, both of which brightened his morning.

"Thanks for what you did," Jordan said.

"I didn't do much. I felt a bit as though I was panicking and being a fussy wife. But when you didn't answer, my imagination went into overdrive. Don't know why. Nana Gloria would say it was the link between us. She might be right at that. Anyway, I'm glad it worked out okay, and I didn't disgrace myself."

"You saved me, love. Don't brush it off. I was in a bind and if Stel and John hadn't turned up when they did, I don't know what would have happened."

Penny's eyes filled with tears, but she turned away, picked up his clothes from the chair and sorted them for the laundry basket. She held up his trousers. "These are a goner, I reckon. So, it's off to the sales next week for you."

Jordan groaned and pulled the duvet over his head. "Don't make me, please. Harry, save me." The little boy might not have understood what was going on, but his mum and dad were happy, so he giggled and burrowed under the covers.

Before she left the room, Penny told him he had a couple of messages. She'd checked them in case they were urgent. Stella had left the details of where they were meeting for breakfast and his old boss had called from the Serious and Organised Crime Team in St Anne Street.

"David Griffiths wants you to ring him back," said Penny. "He'll be in the office until about two, he said. I thought when you left that team you'd be going back to smaller crimes, safer stuff. You know, away from all the guns and gangs. Doesn't seem like it, though, does it?"

"I don't think there's so much of a difference these days. The people Kylie Heywood was mixed up with are undoubtedly linked to bigger fish. So much of the crime tracks back to drugs and trafficking. I'm not going to be involved with that, though. I've passed it on, given them everything I know, and now they can bring in the heavy mob. It's going to be drawn out, I reckon."

"Does it not bother you then? Handing it over when you've done all the work?" she said.

"No. I want to look the bad guys in the eye and see the ordinary people get justice. When I can. You don't get that so much with the multi-force investigations and the international cases. There are so many people involved, and a complicated hierarchy. I'm happier where I am."

Yet again, on the phone, DCI Griffiths tried to talk Jordan into returning to the unit in the city centre. He had held the position unfilled for more than the promised six months and was getting hassle from the management team. Jordan insisted he was happier where he was. "I don't understand," Griffiths said. "You keep unearthing this stuff that we do here, and you know you were valued at St Anne's Street."

"Right now, I'm where I want to be, sir. Really, I appreciate your offer, but this is me, for now at least."

He accepted that the post would need to be filled as soon as they could manage it and had no regret when he finished the call with a promise to meet for a drink in the new year.

Chapter 69

The restaurant in the hotel near to Copy Lane Station was already buzzing when Jordan paused at the entrance looking for Stella. Sales had started in some of the shops in the city and families with bags and boxes gathered round the tables. The bar was lined with drinkers already well into the mood for the New Year celebrations, and the buffet brunch looked very picked over. Children were haring around, getting in the way. Jordan scowled. It would be better to grab a takeaway and go back to the station. Stella was more than ready to agree. She said she'd forgotten how hectic it could be after the years of the pandemic when all of this was off the cards. "It's like a bloody zoo," she said.

They knew where they could buy a decent sandwich, and the coffee machine in the office was soon up and running.

There was paperwork to finish and loose ends to tie up, but the staff had been told that it could wait until Monday. They still had to have the formal interview with Dougie, but in Birkenhead.

Jordan had called John and told him he could take the weekend to spend some time with his family, and they both knew he would probably be with Millie having their own celebration.

They sat in the quiet incident room with just the hum of the station in the background. It would be lively later when the drinking and partying out in the city got underway, but for now there was just a mild sense of anticipation.

Of course, they would discuss the night and the satisfactory outcome. They had a few derogatory words about their colleague from Birkenhead. They agreed he was a bit of a divvy and would probably do well in his career because 'That's what happens.'

Looming over the conversation was Uncle Geoff. Jordan brought up the subject and suggested it was time to move things along in the search. Stella told him she knew he was right, but it felt like a big step. Making it official made it more real for her and she had still been hoping against hope that he would just turn up looking sheepish and things would get back to normal, meaning she wouldn't see him for months. She'd told her grandfather it was all under control, but that was a way of putting it off again. Jordan could see part of it was just fear. Fear that he might have been hurt or worse, or fear that she would find out things she would rather not know. Putting it off wouldn't help, and he had been missing for several days. The murder enquiries had taken precedence, but conscience wouldn't let Jordan turn away again. He brought the paperwork to the table, ready to start the ball rolling.

Stella had programmed her phone with a jingle of *Rudolph the Red-Nosed Reindeer*, but only for certain contact numbers. When the silly noise sounded out, she rolled her eyes.

"Me mam," she said as she held the handset up for Jordan to see.

She mouthed an apology. Jordan shrugged and picked up their cups and, leaving her to the call, went to the coffee machine.

Listening to half of the conversation wasn't interesting, until he saw her leap to her feet and heard her spit out a strong expletive. Jordan spun around to stare at her. Stella was shaking her head and had begun to pace. Jordan frowned at her, and she shook her head again, her eyes wide. She finished the call and slammed the phone on the desktop. Jordan waited for her to gather herself together. She threw her hands in the air and huffed. "Only bloody turned up, hasn't he? Swanned in to Mam's just now, cool as you like, and brought Granda a bottle of Famous Grouse."

"Brilliant," he said.

"What?"

"That's brilliant, isn't it? We know he's okay, we know where he is, and your granddad's got a bottle of whisky. Wins all round."

Stella paused her pacing for a minute and stared at him. "Yeah, you're right, aren't you? Of course, you are. I can go out tonight now without having to worry. I'll tell you what, though, he's going to get a piece of my mind when I go over there. Bloody wally."

"Let's call it a day, Stel. I'm going to Penny's sister's. You're going out with your mates and tomorrow is a new year."

"Yeah. Oh, hang on, that's my phone again." As she extracted the handset from the slew of paperwork, she told Jordan that no matter what, she wasn't going to her mother's for the celebration, so there was no point in her ringing. It hadn't registered that Rudolph had no part in the ring tone, and the number withheld on the little screen drew a puzzled frown. She listened in silence for just a minute before she exploded into threats and warnings; when the call ended, she threw the phone onto the desk. She reached out for the coffee cup; her hand was shaking.

"Everything okay?" Jordan said.

"No, it's bloody not, mate. That was Carl, and that was not a pleasant call at all. In fact, that was very scary and I need to get over to Mam's right now."

Chapter 70

Stella was already pulling her coat on and grabbing her bags from the floor under her chair. "Hey, hang on," Jordan said.

He held up a hand to still her. Although her shoulders were tensed and she was still fastening up her coat and moving away from the desk, he insisted she wait and tell him just what had been said during the phone call.

She took a breath. Counting out on her fingers, she told him that Carl had insisted he knew where Geoff was, that he had known all along. He told her what they didn't know. Her uncle had been hiding out in an Airbnb in Preston and keeping his head down. Carl had laughed, ridiculed her uncle's attempt to hide and was now on his way to Stella's mother's house. The only way to stop him was to give him the money he had been asking for all along. Otherwise, he told her he would blow her precious family wide apart. "I have ten minutes to decide or he's going to tell Granda all about it, he says."

"All about what?"

"What Geoff has been mixed up in. What is behind the blackmail attempt. Dobbing him in to the police? He even said he'd give me the pleasure of that call, and would follow it up with another to Crimestoppers to let them know I had knowledge of a crime. The vile bastard. I don't know what Geoff has been up to and obviously it's going to cause trouble, but not like this. Not with Granda in the middle of it and not right now. Every New Year's Day for the rest of his life, however long or short that might be, he's just going to have the memory of his son getting arrested. He can't do that, Jordan. I can't let him do that."

Although it was obviously their duty to find out what had happened, just what crimes Geoff was guilty of, Jordan could sympathise. It would have to be sorted, but in an organised fashion that gave the family time to process the drama. He stopped for a minute. Would he do this for anyone, any member of the public? Would he hold back? Honestly, probably not.

But this wasn't any member of the public. This was Stella. She spent her time chasing bad guys and making the streets safer. Didn't she deserve a bit of consideration, especially when there didn't seem to be any immediate risk to anyone? Well, anyone except her and her family.

"Did he give you any clue as to just what Geoff has done?"

"No, as I say, he just predicted that it would," – she wiggled her fingers in the air – "'blow my precious family wide open'. What the hell is that supposed to mean?"

Jordan had calmed her enough to stop the rush for the door, but she was pacing back and forth, the phone back in her hand. "I'm going to ring him back. I'm going to tell him that if he makes any move to go to me mam's, I'll swing for him."

"If you do that, he can report you for threatening him. Plus, you really can't communicate with him personally. Shouldn't really have done what we have already done. You know that, don't you? It has to stop."

Stella stared at Jordan. She knew he was right. Without speaking to a higher authority for permission, dealing directly with someone they both knew was a criminal left them open to all sorts of trouble. Jordan made her put the phone into her pocket.

"So, I can't call him. What am I going to do?"

He pulled on his jacket, then sent Penny a text to let her know he would meet her at Lizzie's.

"Come on, let's get this arse and put a stop to him right now."

Chapter 71

Before Stella won the lottery, her mum had lived in a small house in Wavertree. It was where Stella spent her childhood. An ordinary Liverpool semi like hundreds, probably thousands, more. After the win, it had taken a while for Lydia May to decide just where she would like to live. They didn't need to move, but the house was crowded with four generations until Stella had bought a flat for her brother's family. Still, by that time, the idea of moving was firmly entrenched.

She tried to move the family away but after a lifetime living in the same area a relocation to the outskirts simply didn't work. So, bigger, better, and brighter in Wavertree was the final decision and they'd settled down happily, with a nice separate area for Granda and room for visitors. There were green spaces nearby – a playing field, a cricket club – and that was enough countryside to satisfy the older Mays.

In a perfect world, they would be granted a warrant. The technical department would be geared up and ready to track the mobile when Carl Reynolds phoned. Stella would keep him talking, the techies would triangulate the signal and it would be a matter of a few radio messages, blues and twos, and he would be in the hands of the patrol officers in no time. It wouldn't be taken lightly that he had tried to blackmail a police officer.

This was not a perfect world. They didn't have permission to track his phone. It was the early part of New Year's Eve. The technicians were in the pub. The senior officers were strangely not able to be contacted and patrols were on stand-by in case there were any shenanigans with party goers, drunks, or worse – criminals taking advantage of the unusual circumstances of the night.

There was no choice but to head to where they hoped he would be and, if it came to it, to confront him at the family home. After all the effort to protect the old man, it wasn't what either of them wanted, but they were out of options.

Stella and Jordan left Copy Lane. They turned right onto the A59. It was quiet on the roads except for taxis and buses.

At Breeze Hill they took a left and joined Queens Drive. "Stay on this road," said Stella, "but don't go as far as Broadgreen Hospital. The turn is before that, I'll direct you." As she gave him directions, her phone rang, and she stared at the screen for a second. "I think this is him."

"You need to find out just where he is." Even as he said it, Jordan knew the comment was unnecessary. What else was she going to do?

Stella took a breath and clicked the answer button. Jordan could hear the hiss of speech but couldn't make out what was being said. He saw Stella clench her fist on her lap. "You know that's not happening, don't you?" she said. "Just give it up, arsehole. You tried, you failed, now move on."

There was an answering tirade. Stella pointed through the window, indicating the turn onto Prescot Road. "I don't want to hear it, Carl." She was managing to keep her voice low and level, although the words were tough. "You got yourself into a mess, not my problem. You have dirt on Geoff, not my problem. What is your problem, though, mate" – the word dripped with sarcasm – "is that if you upset my granda, I will find you and you'll be sorry you crossed me."

It was all very well Stella besting him in the argument, but this wasn't helping them to find Carl, and Jordan wanted him brought in. There were things about all this that had to be investigated, and just protecting Stella's family wasn't the end of it. Apart from anything else, they would need at some point to justify what they had already done.

She pointed through the window again and they were driving in among the houses. A cold drizzle blurred the view through the windscreen, and Jordan slowed as they passed the entrance to a cricket club. Groups of pedestrians were crossing, heads down, huddled against the weather, over to the low, prefabricated building. Lights and decorations festooned the front, and speakers on the outside blared with music. It contravened all sorts of regulations, but who was going to complain, tonight of all nights?

Stella flapped her hand in an urgent slow-down gesture and Jordan pulled part way onto the pavement and stopped the car. She pushed the button to open her window to halfway and twirled a finger next to her ear. Jordan frowned, not understanding the gesture. She pushed the phone at him and pointed again to the side of her head. He listened in silence and understood.

Wherever he was, Carl was close enough to the cacophony of noise from the party for it to be just audible from his phone.

Chapter 72

Jordan wanted to know how far it was to the Mays' house.

When Stella told him, he reckoned it was too far for the music to have carried, notwithstanding the loudspeakers.

Stella pulled a woolly hat from her pocket and tucked her hair inside. Jordan wished he had something similar, but he turned up his coat collar against the cold blowing rain before he had to leave the warmth of the car.

The cricket field was dark. Behind a low concrete wall and across the narrow access road was a playing field fenced with metal railings. There was no sign of Carl's old Discovery. They passed the noisy building and then turned left and jogged towards the Mays' place. The neighbourhood was mixed. Smaller terraced houses rubbed shoulders with older, grander properties and new-build blocks of flats. There was roadside parking and, with everyone out at gatherings or locked in until the next day, cars were nose-to-tail along the kerb edges. Light from the streetlamps glinted on the wet metal and glass.

Stella pointed to a large, detached house. "That's Mam's." The curtains were open and fairy lights flashed around the window frames. A large Christmas tree stood in the bay on the first floor. Illuminated figures of Disney's Seven Dwarfs pranced across the front garden. There was no sign of Carl Reynolds, and all looked calm. They carried on to the first junction. The music was faintly audible, but would probably not have been picked up on a mobile handset from this distance.

"I reckon he's out in the open," Jordan said. "You wouldn't have heard that music if he was inside the Discovery. No need to look for the car. He must be heading this way. Watch for him on foot." He asked what was behind the house.

"Big gardens and the side fence for the cricket field. Mam's garden isn't huge. It's not her thing."

They could split up and cover more ground or they could stay together for safety. Without speaking, they came down on the side of safety and continued along the road. Jordan pulled the big torch from his pocket, shining the beam over fences and into the dark corners of gardens.

"If he sees us, he'll have it on his toes," Stella said. "Although that'd be good in a way, it doesn't solve the bigger problem."

"No, we need to finish this once and for all. We need to find him. Let's go back to your mum's and wait for him there."

Jordan sensed that the idea of Carl getting so close to the family home made Stella unhappy, but he didn't see any other option. They could easily miss him in the rain-filled darkness. After a moment she nodded, glancing back along the road and just hissing out a one-word expletive.

Turning out the torch, they scuttered back towards the corner, keeping close to the walls and hedges. Once at the house, they split up to cover either side of the junction. The music throbbed in the background and an occasional car hissed past, throwing up pools of standing water, turning them into sheets of rainbow colours with the reflection of the fairy lights.

A small gang of youths crossed the road on their way to the club. They spotted Stella standing by the wall and slowed, pushing at each other and pointing. "All right, love. Stood you up, has he, your fella? Come with us, we'll see you right." They gathered in a group around her. One of the braver ones stepped closer. "Dunno where youse were goin' but you've not got your bling on. Doesn't matter, swerve yer scabby bloke, stick with us. I'll stand yer a few bevvies."

"Move on, lads." Jordan had no choice but to come to her aid. Though he was sure she could have sorted the situation herself, a big black man would have a more instant impact.

"Oh, that's it, like? A white bloke not enough for yer, eh? Stupid cow, your loss."

Jordan stepped closer, looming over the lad who had spoken.

"All right, la. Keep yer hair on. You're welcome to her. Scuzzy bint. Hasn't even put her lippy on for ya."

Sniggering and jeering, they moved away. A couple of them turned to flick one-finger gestures, but they didn't have the heart for a confrontation in the cold and the rain, and while wearing their best clothes.

"Silly sods," Stella said. "I could have handled them."

"I know you could, but we haven't got the time for that sort of thing right now. We don't want to attract attention."

There was a shadow at the edge of his vision and Jordan turned to peer back to the corner where he had been, before the trouble with the lads. The wall was low and obscured by a thick shrub. "There," he said. "In the garden. Can you see?" He turned on his torch as Stella began to run. She struggled with the little metal latch on the gate as it slipped in her cold fingers. Jordan didn't wait but vaulted the wall and onto the grass. Grumpy was felled in the first rush, Sneezy was the next casualty and, as Jordan thrust him aside, the light inside Doc was extinguished.

There was no doubt now that a dark figure was heading around the corner of the house towards the back entrance. Stella had caught up. They didn't want to shout. The family inside were blissfully unaware of the drama in the garden, and they really wanted to keep it that way. There was a short flight of steps down to a basement entrance and Carl Reynolds swung around the edge of the low wall just as Jordan reached him. He turned to take a swing, but Jordan was bigger and faster and leapt the short distance between them to bring the other man down. On a dry day, the result might have been different, but the wet grass was slick underfoot and Jordan's leather-soled shoes had no grip.

As he slipped, he stretched out to grab hold of Carl and snagged his jacket, but the forward motion was too much and the pair of them tumbled to land in a heap in the gritty puddle at the bottom.

Jordan was winded, but Carl had been underneath. His arms had wrapped around Jordan, trying to save himself, so he had no chance to break his fall and protect his head as it bounced off the bricks in the corner.

Stella was there in moments and helped Jordan to clamber to his feet. "You alright, boss?"

"You really need to stop falling down stairs." She laughed until they turned to shine the torch on the heap below them.

"Shit."

Carl Reynolds lay where he had landed on the flagstones. Jordan knelt beside him, feeling for a pulse and talking to the man, rubbing at his chest. Stella was already calling for the paramedics.

"He's got a pulse, he's breathing. There's bleeding from a wound on his head and he's unresponsive right now." Jordan knew the questions the emergency operator would ask and pre-empted them. He pulled off his jacket, which was torn, soaked and dirty, but he tucked it around Carl and leaned over the prone figure, to keep as much of the rain off him as was possible. Stella shrugged out of her coat and between them they held it up as a shelter for the injured man. "Paramedics will get here as soon as they can. Probably about fifteen minutes. Can you manage this cover on your own? I'm going up to get a brolly from Mam, and a tarp or something to keep him dry. Will you be okay?"

"Yes, of course."

She took the stairs two at a time and Jordan heard her thundering on the door and shouting to her mother and brother to get their shit together because she needed help. Soon afterwards there was the clatter of shoes in the dark and then they were there. Blankets, umbrellas, and torches. Lydia was still holding a glass of wine and she glanced down at it with a puzzled expression. She swigged back the booze and placed the glass on the top of the wall.

Carl had still not regained consciousness when the first responder arrived in his fast car. He examined the prone figure, took his pulse, his blood pressure and shone lights into his eyes. He spoke into his radio. "An ambulance is on the way. We'll take him to Walton. It's the best major head trauma centre. Is anyone going to come with him?"

"I'll go." Geoff had been quiet up until now, but he stepped forward. "He's my mate, I'll go."

"You won't," Jordan said. "Sorry, Stel, will you go?"

"Oh, come on, Jordan. It's New Year's Eve. Give her a night off."

Jordan doubted very much that the comment from Stella's uncle was altruistic, and although he felt bad about it, he had no choice.

The scream of the siren precluded any further discussion, and by the time they had Carl on a backboard with a cervical support around his neck, Granda back in the house with a towel and a hot toddy, and Stella in a dry overcoat belonging to her mother, waiting to board the ambulance, Jordan had taken Geoff aside and suggested it would be best if they quietly left the family to themselves and travelled back to Copy Lane.

Chapter 73

Jordan had to find a spare uniformed officer to sit in on the interview. Apart from the reception area, the station was almost empty. The action was all on the streets. In a way, it was a relief when the first thing Geoff did was to ask for a solicitor. They told him that, on this night of all nights, he would have to wait, but he wasn't to be dissuaded and Jordan didn't try too hard. It was a way to leave him to the tender care of the custody sergeant.

The first stop was Walton Hospital, where he found Stella waiting outside the major trauma unit. She was leaning forward, her elbows on her knees, holding a cardboard cup in her hand. The coffee inside was as cold as she was, and just as miserable. She looked up and shrugged as Jordan stood in front of her. She told him they had given her no useful information and, although there had been a scurry of activity at first, everything was going on behind the closed doors. Jordan approached a nurse who was leaning on a counter, talking into a telephone.

Nurses are not much influenced by a police warrant card. They've seen them before and know that often they just bring interruption and hassle. She was polite, though, and scrolled through a screen on the computer when Jordan asked if there was anything of use she could tell him. But, after a minute, she shook her head and closed the monitor. "He's still being assessed, and they are waiting to arrange scans and X-rays and so on."

Jordan glanced at his watch. "Not much going to happen soon then?" he asked.

She gave him the reply he had expected. It was too early to tell, and anything could happen in the next few hours. "He could wake up with a rotten headache or..." She paused, then simply tipped her head to one side and pursed her lips.

A call to the station arranged for a bobby to come and wait at the hospital. "Get off home, Stella," Jordan said. "There's still time to have a couple of drinks. You could make it to your mate's party and see the New Year in at a better place than this."

Stella wanted to know about Geoff, and they agreed to meet up in the morning when the solicitor would likely be available.

The uniformed officer wasn't too bothered about sitting in the hospital. There were people around. It was warm and there was a drinks machine. There were biscuits and chocolates on the nursing station by the door. It was better than a cold, wet street, watching drunks making idiots of themselves.

Jordan had changed into dry clothes in the locker room at Copy Lane and although the casual jacket and jeans were not what he would have chosen for his sister-in-law's dinner party, he knew that him being there would matter more than what he was wearing.

There was just over three quarters of an hour left until the bells when he arrived, to the delight of his wife, and a few snarky comments from her sister. But they gave him a drink and a hot roast-beef sandwich and as midnight loomed closer, he relaxed.

There was champagne and hugs and kisses, and when Harry appeared on the stairs with his cousins, Jordan swooped him up into his arms.

"What's that noise, Dada?"

"It's the foghorns from the boats on the river."

"Why are they doing that?"

"The sailors are happy because it's the New Year."

"Why?"

There are some questions that are just too difficult to answer at midnight with a few stiff drinks inside you and the throbbing from bruises on your back and arms just beginning to ease, so he did the unforgiveable and told his son to 'Ask Mamma,' then passed him over.

Chapter 74

Geoff was unshaven and miserable. He barely raised his head when Jordan and John entered the interview room. They went through the procedure with the recording machine, and the solicitor told them that his client had decided to make a statement against his advice.

He asked where his niece was and grunted when they pointed out that it wouldn't be possible for her to sit in on the interview. They checked that he had been given breakfast and the opportunity to have a shower, and that he was not unwell. He'd been through it all before and answered with dull, monosyllabic responses.

"Okay, what is it you want to tell us, Geoff?" Jordan asked.

Before he answered, he wanted to know how Carl was and they had to tell him they had spoken to the hospital and his friend was in a coma and being monitored. They didn't know when or if he would recover, and made the point that head injuries were difficult to predict.

"He's in the very best place, Geoff. It's a centre of excellence. If anyone can get him right again, they will."

Geoff's response was that as far as he was concerned, it would be best if Carl stayed where he was for the foreseeable future.

"He's brought me nothing but grief. When he turned up again with his big plans, I fell for it. I always do. He's threatened to drop me in it before, I never bloody learn. I've made mistakes, shit, we all have but he's always there, always happy to bring up all the stuff in the past and hold it over my head." He took a breath. "I'll cut straight to the chase. I've got a lock-up. He paid for it, but it's in my name. There's stuff in there. I suppose you'll go and see so I won't bore you with it all. It isn't mine. None of it's mine. It's his, but I don't expect you'll believe me. I'm in shit and I know that. I don't know who he's working with, so don't bother to ask. He was full of it; he was going to make a mint, buy land, go legit and be a developer, but first he had to get some readies. He said if Stella would give me the money, he could get out from under. We could be free of them, whoever 'they' are. We could stop what we were doing. It was always 'we', up to the point when she turned me down. That's when it all got so nasty. What's happened now is her fault, and you tell her that from me."

Carl had told him it was better if he didn't know who was higher up the ladder. "You don't want to know, mate," he'd said. "And they certainly don't want you to know."

Geoff asked for protection and Jordan pointed out that arranging that was far in the future, especially as he had no names for the heavy hitters. There wasn't much to offer in exchange for favours. "We'll see," Jordan told him. "I can't make that decision. Give me something to take to my bosses. The best thing will be if you tell us where your store is and give us the key. Let's get on with this," Jordan said. "I'm not making any promises."

It was a combination lock to a small industrial unit outside Kirkby and it took a couple of hours to assemble a SOCO team, who were not best pleased to be spending New Year's Day examining a warehouse.

Stella insisted on accompanying them and in the end, DCI Lewis gave his permission, providing she didn't touch anything, and the reports were generated by Jordan, the search team, and John. "I don't want her name showing up on anything," he had said, "but I know darned well that if I say no, she'll turn up anyway. At least this way it's under control. Tell her I'm watching her."

It was quiet at the small estate of units. The rain was holding off for a while, but everywhere was damp and cold. Inside the storage unit was dry, though. There was a small electric fan heater in one corner under a picnic table which held a half bottle of whisky and two glasses. The rest of the space was filled with cardboard boxes. Jordan, John, and Stella were left to stew in Jordan's Golf while the SOCOs paraded in wearing their paper suits and booties.

"What do you reckon is in there?" Stella said.

"He wouldn't say. He insisted he didn't know, but that remains to be seen. Could be anything from garden gnomes to smuggled guns. He just said we should come and look; that was it. I have a sneaking suspicion that he doesn't really know, but he has an idea."

"It's not guns. Don't be daft. This is my uncle. Of course it's not guns."

Jordan logged on to his tablet and they watched as video of the search was streamed from inside.

"See, told you it wasn't guns. Bloody hell, has all this been about stupid bloody knock-off anoraks and jeans? What a crock. I always said he had no class. I thought this sort of thing went out years ago, when the docks were pretty much automated, all those containers locked and sealed. Mind you, Jordan, you ripped your jacket and trousers the other day, you could help yourself to some of these. Not really your style, but it'll save you going round the sales."

"I'm going to assume you're joking."

"Course I'm bloody joking. This is tat. I'm disgusted with him. This is not worth going down for. Best that you could do with this stuff is stick it on a stall down the market."

There was nothing to keep them. The stolen goods would be catalogued, and they would have a report in due course. It felt like an anticlimax after all the drama.

"Are we just going to do him for receiving?" Stella wanted to know. But Jordan shook his head. "Let's talk to him first and see what's what. We can't ask Carl, so this could all be fairly protracted if they decide it's worth investigating where this lot came from. Could be from the docks, of course. That might be why Carl wouldn't tell him who was behind it. Could be quite an organisation. Local, possibly. It'll help when we find out where it's come from. My betting is going to be the Far East. Anyway, it's early days."

They were halfway back to the station and a hot cup of coffee when the call came in from the sergeant in charge at Kirkby.

"You need to log back on, boss. There's something you'll want to see. I've sent some footage."

Chapter 75

Back in the office, Jordan booted up his PC, and they gathered round his desk. The video showed the inside of the storage unit; boxes wrapped and labelled, ready for transport, had been moved nearer to the door. White suited figures walked around slowly, occasionally stopping to put down an evidence tent and bag up the odd cigarette end, a lost glove, an empty drink can and then there was a flurry. Two technicians lifted a box that had rested on the cold floor. They juggled with it for a moment as it began to come apart, but in the end, had to let it go as the bottom flopped open. The pile of nylon puffa jackets spread across the floor and they stood for a short while, staring at the mess. With a shrug of his shoulders, one of the figures bent to slide the coats into a pile.

He held up his hand to stop the activity around him and gestured for the video cameraman to come closer. He picked up the jacket and turned it inside out. As they watched, he pulled apart the bottom hem, which had been loosely sewn, and stepped back as small packets fell to the floor at his feet.

"Oh, shit," Stella said.

Jordan's phone rang. "Have you watched it?"

"We have. How much is there?"

"We don't know at this point. We've stopped all activity. There is a lot. We opened a couple of other boxes. It looks like it's mostly pills, but who knows? We need to get the stuff back to a secure location before we can fully investigate. We probably need to call in the NCA."

"It's big enough for that?" Jordan asked.

"I'm afraid it looks like it. It's several coats in each of the boxes we've opened. If all the boxes are involved, it's significant."

"I'll speak to the DCI. I reckon this is going to be taken out of my hands. Hold off everything until we get back to you, okay?"

"Yes, I'm letting some of my crew go home. We'll secure the place and just hang around until we hear more. Try not to take too long, boss. It's brass monkeys here now."

Stella was staring open-mouthed at a still of the packets falling from the hem of the jacket. She looked up, her faced creased in puzzlement. "It can't be. This isn't real. He's a prat and at times an unpleasant prat, but Geoff, a drug trafficker? No."

Jordan wanted to reassure her, but there was nothing he could say. The premises were, by his own admission, in Geoff's name. It would take a better lawyer than the legal aid solicitor who had come in earlier to convince anyone that he didn't know what was in the boxes and where they came from. Maybe it was true but, thankfully, this would not be their responsibility anymore. He thought of his earlier conversation with Penny about how much circled back to the evils of drugs. The deaths of innocent sick and old people, probably the slide into lawlessness by Kylie Heywood and the dire situation that Carl Reynolds was now in. Separate issues but connected by the need for money and the hope of a quick fix.

There were calls to be made, and explanations. They arrested Geoff on suspicion of trafficking. They had no choice, although he denied any knowledge and insisted all he had done was carry the boxes in from the back of a van and stack them in the unit. Bail was out of the question. He'd vanished once before, and he was a flight risk for certain. He protested his innocence but still couldn't or wouldn't give them names without the promise of protection.

It was very late in the day before everything had been organised. The boxes were on their way to a secure facility and the job of examining all the coats and recording the contents of the hidden packets was underway. It had already been handed over to St Anne Street and the Serious and Organised Crime Team. It was out of their hands and time to call it a day.

"I'll have to tell Granda," Stella said. "He needs to know as soon as possible, and I want to be the one. I can answer all his questions without too much drama."

"Do you want me to come with you?" Jordan asked as they crossed the car park.

"No, I'll do it. I've rung to say I was coming. I've warned them the news is not good, so all it needs now is for me to minimise the shock and prepare them for what's next."

* * *

It was a difficult conversation. There were tears and questions, and some ranting and swearing. Lydia May cursed her brother and insisted she'd always known he'd come to no good. In the end, she was persuaded to take herself off, red faced and teary-eyed, to the kitchen to make something to eat. Stella stayed in the living room, surrounded by the after-Christmas glitter, which seemed more faded and sadder than in other years. Her granddad sat by the fire with a glass of whisky and stared at the flickering gas flames. There was the glint of moisture in his eyes. She had tried so hard to spare him this, but it had been inevitable all along.

"Are you okay, Granda?" she said.

"Aye, I am."

"I'm sorry about Geoff."

"What are you sorry for?"

"You know he's going to go to jail, possibly for a good while?"

"Yes. I know. It was only ever a matter of time. He was a scally from way back. We did our best, me and your nan, but some people just can't be helped. The main thing is that you're okay. That you didn't get into trouble. You didn't, did you?"

"No, I didn't do anything wrong. So, you're okay with it all?"

"I wish it hadn't happened. Course I do, but he's made his bed and he'll lie in it. We'll be here for him when he gets out, but he'll never do much good now. You're the one."

"How do you mean?"

"You're the best of us. I can't tell you how proud I am of you, Queen."

"Aw, Granda." She leaned over and hugged him tight so that he couldn't see the tears.

"And that fella you're with. I like him, you know, in spite of–" he waved a hand in front of his face "–and we didn't meet under the best of circumstances."

"Which fella?"

"That one that's named after a river. What is he, erm?"

"Oh, do you mean, Jordan? God, Granda, I'm not with him. Not like that, anyway. He's my boss. He's married. I know his wife and everything."

"Aye, that's as maybe, but I'm an old codger. I see what I see. Now get out, footie's on in five. Go on, get off home and have some fun with your mates."

As Stella left, he took a big handkerchief from his cardigan pocket and blew his nose. She didn't wait to speak to the rest of them. She needed to be in her own space.

* * *

Jordan and Penny were in front of the fire with a glass of rum each and the rest of the special chocolates. He suggested a trip away, maybe up to Scotland for some skiing if the snow came. Penny told him she was up for that if he wanted to, but right then she was happy where she was.

The End

List of characters

Detective Inspector Jordan Carr — Jamaican heritage. Married to Penny. They have one child, called Harry. Lives in Crosby.

Lizzie — Penny's sister.

Detective Sergeant Stella May — Liverpool born and bred. Lives in Aintree.

Lydia May — Stella's mother. Lives in Wavertree with her father.

Peter May — Stella's brother.

Nana Gloria — Jordan's granny.

Geoff May — Stella's uncle.

Carl Reynolds — Geoff's dodgy mate.

DCI David Griffiths — Detective Chief Inspector with Serious and Organised Crime.

Keith Young — Stella's neighbour. Tenant of the upstairs flat. Physiotherapist at the Royal Hospital.

Detective Constable John Grice — Newly promoted detective. Boyfriend of Millie from the technical laboratory.

DCI Josh Lewis – Detective Chief Inspector in charge at Copy Lane.

Kath Webster – Junior officer who is waiting for a knee replacement.

Violet Purcell – Junior officer. Has spent all her working life in the force and is retiring in five years.

Karen – DCI Lewis's secretary.

Ted Bliss – Crime scene sergeant.

Sergeant Flowers – Crime scene manager, acerbic and sarcastic.

Dr James Jasper – Medical examiner based at the University of Liverpool and Liverpool Central Morgue.

Phyllis Grant – Medical examiner.

Vickie Frost – SOCO sergeant.

Stan and Tracy Lipscowe – Victims.

Florence McGrady – Lipscowes' neighbour.

Musa Rahanov – Printer in Walton Vale. Chechnyan.

Tony Yates – Lipscowes' neighbour.

Frank Dirkin – Lipscowes' neighbour.

Joan and Peter Lester – Victims.

Detective Sergeant Andy Campbell – Newly transferred to Birkenhead major crime team.

Detective Chief Inspector George Harkness – DS Andy Campbell's boss in Birkenhead.

Kylie Heywood – Suspect.

Brian Boland – Suspect.

Dougie Waters – Suspect.

If you enjoyed this book, please let others know by leaving a quick review on Amazon. Also, if you spot anything untoward in the paperback, get in touch. We strive for the best quality and appreciate reader feedback.

editor@thebookfolks.com

www.thebookfolks.com

Other titles of interest

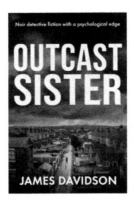

OUTCAST SISTER by James Davidson

London detective Eleanor Rose is lured back to her home
city of Liverpool by Daniel, an ex-boyfriend and colleague
who's in danger. But when she retraces his steps to a grim
housing estate, he's nowhere to be found. Has she walked
into some kind of trap? Is Rose ready to confront the
demons she finds there?

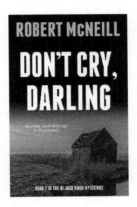

DON'T CRY, DARLING by Robert McNeill

The Edinburgh major crimes team is on high alert after a
shooting at a card game leaves three people dead. But the
officers must divide their focus when the daughter of a
prominent figure goes missing. Can DI Knox catch her
abductor before the unthinkable happens, and stop a
dangerous killer in his tracks?